Teen Superheroes Book Three:

The Battle for Earth

Copyright 2012 Darrell Pitt

Find out more about Darrell at his website:

http://www.darrellpitt.com

Email: darrellpitt@gmail.com

Dedicated

To Rob Ashe

Teen Superheroes

Book Three

The Battle for Earth

Prolog

Here's what's happened so far.

We're a bunch of teenage superheroes. Sounds strange? You should try being us. We were the victims of an experiment carried out by a secret organization known only as The Agency. Our memories were wiped and we were given amazing powers—and new identities.

My name is Axel. I can control air. I can use it to help me fly, or I can create shields to protect me from a hail of bullets, or I can create a tornado. I'm American, but as to exactly where I was from—well, don't ask because I don't know. That's what happens when someone wipes your memory.

Chad is from Norway. He has the ability to create—and manipulate—fire and ice. He's also a pain in the—well, you can guess. He's a friend, but the kind of friend you want to lock in a closet sometimes so you can watch television in peace.

His sister's name is Ebony. She can transmute one substance into another. She's quieter than her brother, but I think she's gained a lot of confidence in a short time. You can't stay quiet for long when you deal with super villains and monsters on a daily basis.

Then there's Brodie. She's my girlfriend. Mostly. Sometimes she wants to hit me over the head, but love does strange things to you. Originally from Australia, she has the strength and agility of three grown men as well as being a master of martial arts.

The youngest member of our team is Dan. He can manipulate metals—and sometimes even minds. He's from China. He likes to think of himself as being like Luke Skywalker, but he's probably a little more like Yoda.

Don't tell him I said that.

That leaves Ferdy. He's a genius in addition to being immensely strong. He's also autistic, so he's a little hard to understand sometimes. Still, he's one of us. He's part of our family so if you mess with him, you mess with all of us.

Let me set the record straight on a couple of things. We don't have superhero names or wear crazy outfits. We're currently living at the Las Vegas compound of The Agency. The organization is headed up by a race of aliens known as the Bakari. The head of our branch is named Twenty-Two.

Yes, that's his name.

One day we want to find our families—if we have families—and we want our memories back.

Is that too much to ask?

Chapter One

This is my lucky day, Brian Hendrix thought.

He had only been sitting at the bar of The Purple Monkey for an hour when a beautiful, unattached woman walked through the door into the dark interior. She positioned herself at the corner of the bar and gazed at him once before ordering a drink and turning her attention to the television above the counter.

He shot a single look in her direction.

That glance told him two things. The first was that she was astonishingly attractive. Slim physique. Black, raven hair. Green eyes. A real stunner. His second thought was that she was out of his league.

Way out of his league.

He turned his attention to the mirror behind the bar. Behind the assorted bottles of liqueurs and spirits, he caught a glimpse of himself and saw a man, fifty years old, twenty pounds overweight and balding. He focused on the bald spot. He was *very* balding. The top of his head would be completely hairless by the time he turned fifty-five. Probably sooner.

Still, some women found bald men attractive. Look at Bruce Willis.

Glancing sideways, he realized the woman's eyes were again directed straight at him. He diverted his attention to the television positioned above the bar.

She must be a hooker, he thought.

Of course. She would be pleasant and accommodating and probably interested in a fancy and furious fling—but money would have to change hands. Brian self-consciously stroked his wedding ring. Elizabeth was everything a perfect wife could be. Faithful. Supportive. Loving. She had given him two sons. Both fine young men.

As for himself…

While he had been a good provider, he had not always been the ideal husband. Not that there had been a new woman in every town. Far from it. There had been no more than three or four other women over the years. Well, certainly no more than a dozen.

'Wow,' the woman said. 'Check that out.'

Brian almost dropped his glass. He had been looking at the television without focusing. Now he watched the screen as an enormous metal monster—some sort of robot—picked up a car and threw it across a street. The footage was being broadcast live. A line of text ran across the bottom of the screen.

Giant Robot Runs Rampant in Las Vegas. Two confirmed dead. Dozens injured.

Six months ago he would have thought the television was tuned to the Disney Channel, but the world was a different place now.

Mods, Brian thought. *The whole world's become a freak show.*

Most people refused to believe that mods existed—even with television coverage and appearances on Ellen and other talk shows—until they witnessed a mod for themselves. For a long time Brian had quietly been one of the conspiracy theorists who suspected that mods were some sort of government-inspired delusion. That until he spent a week in New York and saw a man flying across the Brooklyn Bridge.

Flying.

With no plane.

Brian had found himself looking for a jet pack or wires when suddenly the small figure started shooting bolts of lightning from his fingers. Through sheer luck, Brian had survived the experience. A man standing next to him had not been so lucky. One of the lightning bolts struck him and turned him to charcoal. As Brian dove for cover behind a car he found himself shaking and crying all at once. It was true. *They were real.* Half an hour later another flying man in tights had taken out Lightning Man. The papers described the duo as a super villain and a superhero, but Brian knew them as something else.

'Freaks,' he said. 'Goddamn freaks of nature.'

He had not meant to say the words aloud, but he found the woman nodding her head enthusiastically at him.

'I used to feel safe,' she said. 'But now…'

Brian nodded. He related his story to the woman, leaving out his ensuing fit of hysteria at the hospital.

'That must have been terrible,' the woman sympathized.

'Worst day of my life,' Brian said. 'That poor man just burst into flame. Horrible.'

'Morgan.'

'Huh? Whassat?'

'My name is Morgan. Morgan Jones.'

She held out her hand. Brian shook it and introduced himself. 'I'm in insurance.'

'That must be interesting,' Morgan said.

Now Brian knew the woman *had* to be a hooker. No-one thought insurance was interesting. No-one. Still, she seemed friendly enough. Now Brian started wondering how much she charged for female companionship. His family life seemed a long way away now.

'I'm not a hooker,' Morgan said. 'In case that's what you're thinking.'

'Not at all.' Brian tried to look shocked. 'The thought had not crossed my mind.'

'I just thought I'd come here for a quiet drink. My husband passed away recently.'

'I'm sorry to hear that.'

'It was cancer. Probably for the best...' She saw his puzzled expression. 'I mean, the world's gone crazy. What with all these flying people about...'

'I know what you mean.' Brian nodded vigorously. 'There should be laws. The government's gotta make them illegal. Shoot 'em on sight.'

'Absolutely.'

Brian started to put together the pieces of what Morgan had told him. Here she was, a beautiful woman grieving for her husband, probably feeling a little lonely, a little confused, probably seeking someone to talk to. Maybe wanting a little comforting—

'I have a bottle of rather good French Bordeaux back in my hotel room,' Morgan said. 'Are you partial to red wine?'

At that moment Brian would have nodded enthusiastically if she had suggested drinking petrol. He gave the barman a good tip—making certain that Morgan saw the generous amount—and followed her outside.

'I'm staying at the Winstead Arms just up the street.' She pointed. 'I don't like the hotel knowing my business. Would you mind waiting a few minutes before you come up?'

'Not at all.'

She handed him a swipe key to her room and told him she was staying in room eleven-sixteen. She would be waiting for him. Brian watched the beautiful woman walk down the sidewalk away from him. If she hadn't just handed him a card to her room, he would have thought she was dumping him. Of course, maybe it wasn't the key to her room at all. Maybe it was just some old library card.

Brian counted off the minutes before starting down the street after her. He found the hotel without difficulty, marched briskly past the main desk and punched the elevator button without glancing over at reception. He made his way to the floor and stopped outside of the room. His hands shook as he swiped the card. The light above the panel turned green.

Bingo, he thought. *I knew it was my lucky day.*

'Morgan?' he called.

'In the living room,' her voice responded.

Brian closed the door behind him and walked down a short corridor. The woman stood in the middle of the room. Now Brian noticed something very strange. The entire room was covered in plastic as if it were being painted. And it reminded him of something else. What was it?

Dexter. That freak serial killer always spread out plastic before he killed somebody.

'What—?' He stopped in his tracks.

'Did they see you down at reception?' she asked.

'Yes.' Brian's heart was beating wildly, but now it was from trepidation. Still, this was a single, unarmed woman. There was no reason why he couldn't safely extricate himself from this situation. 'I spoke to them. They know—'

'You didn't speak to them.' Morgan shook her head slowly. 'You didn't say anything to them at all, Brian. You were a good boy. Weren't you?'

Brian tried to speak, but he found he could not open his mouth. *What the hell—?* His jaw would not move. Now he tried to run, but his legs would not work. It was as if they were plastered to the floor.

'Come over here,' Morgan said.

Against his will, he found himself walking across the plastic sheeting. He tried to scream, but he seemed to have completely lost control of his body. A sudden realization struck him. This woman was some kind of mod. *A freak!*

She seemed to be able to read his mind. 'My real name is Morgan Le Fay. You may have heard my name in conjunction with Arthurian legend. The ancients seemed to regard me as some kind of witch.' She shook her head and smiled sadly. 'I'm too pretty to be a witch.'

Brian tried with all his might to scream.

'You'll have to forgive me,' Morgan continued. 'You see, I've eaten so many people over the centuries that there remains no joy in the consumption.'

Brian's eyes opened with horror.

'Now the only joy remains in the preparation of the meal.' Morgan could have been talking about cooking lasagne for dinner. 'Now, be a good boy and open your mouth.'

Brian felt his lips being forced apart.

'Wider,' Morgan instructed.

His mouth opened wider and still he could not make a sound.

'You have lovely lips,' Morgan said. She placed a forefinger against his bottom lip and for a single, entrancing second Brian was captured again by her beauty. But only for a second. For she then slid her slender hand into his mouth, formed a fist and punched it straight down his esophagus.

Brian felt a shudder of immense agony as the interior of his throat was ripped apart and the bones in his neck shattered. His eyes started to roll up into his head.

'Oh, please no,' Morgan soothed. 'Don't die too quickly.'

But much to her disappointment, before she had torn off his arms and legs, before she had even begun to consume him, Brian Hendrix's eyes stared into nothing and his heart had thudded to a shuddering halt.

'Disappointing,' Morgan said. 'Not my lucky day at all.'

Chapter Two

'Unlucky us.' I peered down over the city. 'Why do we end up with all the weirdos?'

The robot stood as high as a city building. It looked vaguely like a giant spider, although it had only six legs and was made from a variety of shiny metals. Its body was circular in shape whereas its head was a perfect oval. At the front of that oval lay a wide, black windshield. Behind it, presumably, sat the crazy person in charge of the monster.

We were in a Flex Fighter, zooming in low over the city. There were five of us in the aircraft: myself, Chad, Dan, Ferdy and Ebony. Brodie had gone shopping earlier that day and she had not answered any of the frantic calls made to her cell. Obviously she had her phone off and her wallet open. This hadn't worried me, but Agent Palmer—our immediate supervisor at The Agency—had not been happy.

I stared down at the monstrosity, glad that Brodie would not have to face this creature.

'How big is that thing?' Ebony asked.

The thin, blonde girl hovered at my elbow.

'It's over fifty feet tall,' Chad replied. 'Maybe a hundred.'

'It's nothing Team Incredible can't handle,' Dan said.

The four of us looked at him. Dan had been coming up with names for our group for months. Some of them had quite a ring to them, but this one had about as much tune to it as a garbage bin thrown down a flight of stairs.

'Team Incredible,' Ebony echoed. 'Wow. I wonder if that's already copyrighted.'

'Ferdy will help.' Ferdy's eyes were fixed on the giant robot. 'Ferdy can smash the robot into pieces.' He peered through the window. 'The Titanic sank on the twelfth of April, nineteen hundred and twelve.'

'Sure, Ferdy,' I said. Ferdy's autism made him difficult to work with sometimes. Trying to battle a giant robot could prove dangerous. 'We'll see how things pan out.'

I peered back down at the robot below. It had

appeared only minutes earlier on the famous Sunset Strip, burrowing its way out of the ground like some sort of enormous groundhog. It had begun by picking up cars and flinging them about like toys before turning its attention to the famous Luxor Hotel.

Already, the mighty obelisk and the one hundred and ten foot high recreation of the Great Sphinx had been reduced to rubble. Now the metal creature lumbered across the wreckage towards the mighty pyramidal-shaped hotel.

'There are thousands of people within that building,' I said. 'If it crashes into the Luxor—'

'Bring us in to land,' Ebony ordered the Flex.

The voice-activated aircraft immediately swooped in low and settled close to the scene. The aircraft was a new experimental design; its computer system operated via a new bionugenic gel. It was supposedly faster and more responsive than any other craft developed by The Agency. The back of the aircraft opened and we piled out into the midst of a debris-ridden street. Several vehicles had been thrown into nearby buildings. A tourist bus lay on its side.

Bodies were strewn all over the road. Smoke began to billow from the interior of the transit vehicle.

'That bus has still got people in it,' Chad said.

'I'll see to it.' Ebony grabbed Ferdy's arm. 'You come with me.'

Good, I thought. *We'll focus on the robot.*

We raced through the debris towards the enormous metal creature. It had almost reached the mighty hotel. I could see people streaming out of the structure as the sound of an alarm drifted distantly through the warm air. It looked like a full-scale evacuation was in progress.

'We need to stop that thing,' I said.

'I'll get its attention,' Chad said.

He drew back his arm and formed a fist. As he punched, we saw an enormous ball of ice form in mid-air and fly directly towards the robot. It smashed into the back of its oval head, bringing it to a halt. The robot turned about with amazing speed, its head finally focusing on us.

'I think that worked,' Dan said.

Two machine guns jutted out of its mouth.

'Look out!' I yelled.

I threw up an air shield as it fired, and the bullets ricocheted harmlessly away from us.

'We need to split up!' Chad said.

That was the last thing I felt like doing, but he raced away before I could reply. Chad not only had the power to control fire and ice, but he also had to ability to be incredibly annoying! And he did it so easily! There were times I would have happily unleashed a metal robot on him myself.

I cast a helpless glance at Dan. He shrugged and raced off in the other direction. Great. Instead of organizing a co-ordinated assault—as we had practiced hundreds of times in training—we were attacking the creature separately.

Really clever.

I started forward. Fortunately, the robot seemed mostly focused on me, firing intermittently in my direction. My shield held. Over the last few months I had suffered problems with my powers. My abilities inexplicably—and usually at the worst times—would suddenly cut out. Doctor Williams, a scientist back at The Agency, had been examining me without coming to any conclusions. Fortunately my powers had not failed at a vital time.

Not yet, anyway.

I built up a burst of hurricane wind and flung it at the creature. It barely impacted the creature. In fact, its only response was to retract the gun barrels. A single, long barrel appeared and pointed directly at me.

Oh, oh.

The cannon fired. I had my shield up, but the blast of it still threw me backward. Colliding with a section of broken wall, I hit my head and my vision shuddered slightly. Whoever built that thing certainly knew how to pack a wallop.

Clambering to my feet, I built up another concentrated burst of wind, but before I could fire it I saw pieces of metal rocket through the air towards the robot. Balls of fire began to batter it from the other. Obviously the others had begun their attack.

The robot responded by swinging its head about and firing at them. Chad and Dan were beyond my range of vision; hopefully they were hidden somewhere among the enormous piles of rubble. I started forward again.

Firing a blast of wind at the creature had not affected it at all. I wondered if a single, focused gust might be enough to do some damage. I created a sphere of air the size of a cannonball and aimed it at the head of the creature. This time I saw it shudder under the impact.

Mind you, it shuddered. That doesn't mean it rolled onto its back and died, because it didn't. The three of us continued our attack, but the robot merely retaliated by alternating its fire between the three of us. I caught a glimpse of Chad taking refuge behind a pile of debris. Normally he acted as if he could take on the world himself—hell, sometimes I thought his head was the size of a planet—but even he looked concerned.

'Chad!' I yelled. 'Freeze the leg! The leg!'

Chad looked up, saw me and nodded. He pointed at the leg nearest him and within seconds it had turned white. This was a new technique we had been practicing. Normally he just produced ice. Instead, he had been training to produce its companion—cold.

'Do it!' he yelled.

I fired another blast. Aiming for the leg, this time the limb instantly shattered into thousands of pieces. The robot stumbled. Discus-sized pieces of metal crashed into the other front leg of the creature. I still could not see Dan, but he had obviously guessed our strategy. Within seconds the second limb collapsed under the creature.

Still, the monster had plenty of fight left in it. Whereas it had relied purely on its weaponry to take us out, now it turned to good old-fashioned brute force. It staggered straight towards me. I turned to jump out of its way, but one of its legs struck me a glancing blow and I hit the ground. It raised its leg again. I rolled out of the way just as its claw foot slammed down.

Crunch!

The limb lifted again and came crashing down. This time I rolled to the left. It missed me. I had to get up and get away from here, but there was debris on all sides. I formed a barrier as the leg arrowed directly towards me.

I let out a cry. The claw foot was pushing against my shield. It was three feet from my face. Two feet. Now only inches—

The entire robot shuddered and stopped. I heard the sound of an explosion; the leg lifted and I watched in amazement as the entire creature toppled to one side.

What had happened?

Dan appeared. 'Did you see that? I must have hit its control mechanism!'

'That's good, Dan,' I said.

Slowly rising to my feet, I felt a little embarrassed. Dan was the youngest of our group, but it looked like he had finished off the monster. I saw a row of disks had impacted the creature's side. One of them must have hit a vital system.

Chad raced over.

'Did you see that?' he asked. 'Frozen one second! Toast the next! Yet another bad dude brought down by The Chad!'

The Chad?

'Brought down—' Dan was speechless. 'I'm the one who finished it off.'

'You? Don't be ridiculous, punk. It was me who—'

This was one argument I wasn't getting into.

'You both did great,' I said. 'Now we need to find the clown who was operating this thing.'

That didn't take long. Within minutes we had found a rear hatch to the robot. Dan used his metal manipulation abilities to wrench open the doorway. Inside, we found a small man wearing glasses cowering behind his control seat.

'I'm Doctor Robot!' he screamed. 'I'm the greatest super villain the world has ever seen!'

'You're an idiot,' I told him. 'One of many.'

We took him back to the street and handed him over to the police. The officers didn't bother asking our names. They knew we wouldn't tell them and it was a waste of time. I could see the media in the distance. It was best if we got moving.

We headed in Brodie and Ferdy's direction. It looked like they'd been busy. The tourist area was a scene of utter chaos. Debris all over the road was making it difficult for emergency service operators to get to all the injured. The fire on the burning bus had been put out and the passengers evacuated. I caught Ferdy's eye. He was kneeling next to a man lying in a twisted heap on the street.

I hurried over to them.

'This man is hurt,' Ferdy said. 'He is bleeding.'

I knelt next to the stranger. He was covered in blood. It looked like Ferdy—or someone—had applied a makeshift bandage to his wound, but blood was still flowing. The man tried to speak and I gently took his hand.

'Help is on the way,' I said. 'The ambulance officers are almost here.'

'Not…going to make it…not…' the man tried to speak.

'You're going to be fine. Just hold on.'

It was a lie and I knew it. Within seconds the

man's eyes fluttered and a single tear ran down one side of his face. He stared up at the sky without comprehension.

A hollowness opened up within me. At the edges of that hollow feeling lingered hot anger. I didn't know this man, but he was someone's son. Maybe he had a wife and family. Now he would never see his family again because fate had placed him in the wrong place at the wrong time.

I arranged the stranger's hands on his chest and wiped the single tear from his face.

The ambulance officers arrived a few seconds later.

Too late. Far too late.

I felt numb as Ferdy and I walked back to the Flex Fighter. As we drew near, Ferdy stopped and placed a hand on my shoulder.

'The man died,' he said.

'Yes. He died.'

'Approximately one hundred and fifty thousand people die each day.'

I nodded absently. 'If you say so.'

'You wiped the tear from the man's face,' Ferdy persevered. 'You straightened his clothing. You laid his hands on his chest.'

I looked down at my own hands. They were covered in the stranger's blood. I had seen people die before now—I had even been the cause of some of their deaths. Still, there was no getting used to seeing a person lose their life.

'The man deserved respect,' I said. 'He may have had a wife…a family…'

'But he was dead.' Ferdy looked confused. 'He could not know you would wipe the tear from his face. He could not know—'

'Ferdy. How you die has got to be at least as important as how you live. It has got to mean something.'

We made our way back to the Flex in silence. I wasn't sure if Ferdy had understood me. We climbed aboard the aircraft. No-one said anything much as the plane lifted up into the sky. I closed my eyes as we were swept away from the devastation and arced across the city towards the desert.

Chapter Three

'I heard it got rough out there,' Agent Palmer said.

They were the first words she said after we landed. She had been monitoring the situation via news reports. The Flex Fighter had come in to land in a cave located at the southern end of a small valley away from the lights of Las Vegas. From here, a high speed transporter would return us to the heart of the city.

'It was nothing I couldn't handle,' Chad said. 'I am, after all, a superhero.'

'You are, after all, an idiot,' Ebony said.

Chad shook his head in dismay. 'My own sister mocks me.'

'With good reason,' she said.

Agent Palmer caught my eye. 'How are you?' she asked.

'Okay.'

'Really?'

'There was a lot of carnage out there today.' I couldn't get the dead man's face out of my mind. 'A lot of people got killed.'

'A lot more would have been killed if you hadn't been there.' The agent turned to everyone. 'Well done. These sorts of crazies seem to be on the increase.'

She didn't need to tell us that. Ever since the United Nations had announced that mods were on Earth—and had been for centuries—there seemed to be some new threat every day. It had made me wonder more than once if our existence wouldn't have been better kept a secret.

We made our way over to what appeared to be a normal elevator. I climbed in with a sigh. I wanted a shower; the dead man's blood was still all over my hands. The others looked a mess as well. The lift started off with a slight pull; we were moving in a sideways direction at several miles per hour. How the thing operated without plastering us to the back of the lift was beyond me. It worked. That was all that mattered to me. Just as long as I didn't have to walk back to town. Anything was better than that.

Palmer drew me to one side as soon as we

piled out of the elevator.

'Twenty-Two wants to see you,' she said. 'Just as soon as you clean up.'

What would the alien commander want with me?

'I have no idea,' Palmer replied when I asked her. 'Could be the length of your hair. It is getting a little long.'

Yeah. Sure.

A few minutes later I was back in my hotel room and washed, dried and reclothed. My room was on the fourth floor of a hotel in the middle of Las Vegas. Beneath the building lay the infrastructure of The Agency—meeting rooms, training centers, communications rooms. It was a massive complex. Even I had only seen a small part of it. The hotel enabled us to carry out a normal life—or as normal a life as you can have when you're working as a genetically modified superhero for a secret organization.

I climbed into an elevator and descended back down into the burrows of The Agency. Twenty-Two's office was several floors beneath street level. It lay at the end of a concrete corridor where a female receptionist sat typing at a computer. I tried to remember her name. I couldn't.

'I'm here to see Twenty-Two,' I said.

'Your name?' the girl asked.

And here I was thinking I was famous.

'Axel,' I said. 'Smith.'

She spoke into a phone for a moment. 'Twenty-Two will see you now.'

I entered his office.

Twenty-Two looked about as ordinary as anyone else. He was tall, thin and bald. Possibly they forgot to tell him about hair when he was instructed on how to look like a human. I had no idea as to the true appearance of the Bakari. Whatever they really looked like, they probably bore little resemblance to a human.

I had seen him around other parts of The Agency complex, but we had not officially met and I had never seen him outside the building.

Maybe the Bakari were allergic to sunlight.

Who knew?

'Axel.' His voice was warm. He sounded so human. Still, I felt a shiver dance along my spine. I had only met one other Bakari. He was known as Twelve—don't ask me about why they had numbers for names—and he had been responsible for the experimentation carried out on us. Later he had tried to kill us.

I tried to remind myself that this man was a different alien and that was a different time.

It wasn't easy.

'Please take a seat,' Twenty-Two said.

I slid into a chair. 'What's this all about?'

'I wanted to keep you apprised as to developments regarding your family.'

It took a moment for this to sink in. My family. That's right. A million years ago Agent Palmer had said The Agency was trying to track down information regarding our true identities. Maybe even reconnect us with our families—if we had any.

I had been told I had a brother, but I had

driven this information as far from my mind as possible. After everything that had happened to us, the possibility of a brother was too much to hope for.

Still…

'What have you found out?' I asked.

'Our enquiries have been inconclusive, but we are following a trail of information to its source.'

'What sort of trail?'

'As you know, most of the records regarding the Alpha Experiment were destroyed by the scientists involved and then later by Twelve.'

I nodded. Evil aliens don't like leaving a trail.

'However,' Twenty-Two continued. 'It appears there were some hard copies of documents that were missed. We have people examining them now.'

'Do you think—' I found I could not speak. 'What are the chances—'

'We don't know,' the alien said. 'It will take some time to sort out.'

'I see.'

'Anyway, I just wanted to let you know.'

I looked up and realized the meeting was abruptly at an end. Fine. I stood up, shook Twenty-Two's hand again and left the office. Ignoring the girl at the desk, I made my way through the complex to the main concourse of The Agency. This level had been redesigned the previous month. It was now the size of a football field, with communications screens surrounding the exterior. A park, complete with artificial trees and lawn, filled the center. It had been christened The Hub.

My phone rang. I glanced at the display.

Brodie.

I had forgotten all about her. Hitting the receive button, I realized she had sent a message with an attached file.

What was this all about?

Not more handbags, I hoped. The Agency gave us an allowance and Brodie's handbag collection had been increasing at the rate of one per week. If I had to look at another handbag—

I opened the first image. It showed Brodie lying still on a floor. After staring at the image in horror for what seemed like an eternity, the image was replaced by a series of words. They began:

You will follow our instructions to the letter if you want this girl to live.

Chapter Four

Brodie awoke to find her face pressed against a cold metal floor. Her head hurt. Why did her head hurt? It was hard to think. The last thing she could remember was walking down East Charleston Boulevard. Someone had come up behind her. She had turned around, thinking it was some mugger, and then—

Then everything had turned green.

Green.

That was not a good sign. She slowly sat up. She was in a metal room. A *grimy* metal room. It was obviously some sort of cell, and judging by the sway of the chamber, she was on board a ship.

How the hell had she ended up here?

And why?

There was no window in the room so it was impossible to tell if it was day or night. She checked for her phone. Gone. So there was no way to call for help.

Still, whoever had kidnapped her may not know about her enhanced strength or fighting abilities. She went to the door of the cell. Also constructed from metal, it had some sort of complicated electronic locking mechanism. She had never seen anything like it.

Brodie peered around the cell, her eyes finally settling on a metal box set into the wall near the lock. Burying her fingers into the groove around the edge of it, she pulled hard and broke off the cover. A series of blue and orange leads wrapped in translucent silver filaments filled the box. She dragged at the wires.

Bang!

A shower of sparks erupted from the interior and Brodie released the wires.

'Kids,' she murmured to herself. 'Don't try this at home.'

She grabbed the wires again and dragged them across to the electronic lock. Keeping her hands free from the ends, she took a deep breath and touched the ends to the electronic display. This time there was no sound, but the display flickered a few times before failing completely.

'Yes!' She dropped the wires, pulled at the

door and opened it easily. 'Escape à la Brodie!'

She peered into the hallway. Despite the grimy appearance of the flooring and walls, this was obviously some sort of high tech ship and she was stuck in the bowels of it. She would have to try to get above deck without being seen and then steal a rowboat or send a mayday.

Great.

And all she wanted was a new handbag.

Still, no-one ever said the life of a superhero was meant to be easy. Not that she really thought of herself as a superhero. She just happened to be an Australian girl with three times the strength and speed of a normal man, a multitude of martial arts abilities, and an employee of a secret agency operating within the United States.

If that made her a superhero, then—

Actually, she thought. *That probably does make me a superhero.*

Still, she wished Axel were here. A pang of emotion gripped her chest. She might have superpowers, but she was also a girl. She found herself thinking about Axel all the time although she was not sure he felt the same way. He often seemed preoccupied with other things.

Brodie drove the thoughts from her mind. Now was the time for action, not for girly-girly-mush-mush. She hurried down the corridor. There seemed to be doors on both sides—possibly other people were imprisoned within—but she couldn't do anything about them right now. She had to focus on escaping.

The corridor ended with a set of stairs heading upward. Racing up them, she found herself facing another set of stairs and a passageway identical to the one she had just left. Up had to be the best direction. Brodie ascended again and reached another corridor, but now the stairs had run out. Making her way along the passageway, she sighted an elevator at the end. There were strange symbols on the display.

What language is that? She didn't recognize it. The up button was the only thing that mattered and it was obvious enough. She pushed it and waited.

A few seconds passed. The doors opened

and—

Brodie's mouth fell open. The occupant of the elevator was over six feet in height, covered in scales and had a face not unlike that of a fish; its eyes were placed back on the sides of its head. The hairless creature fell back in surprise as it stared in astonishment at Brodie. Its mouth fell open to reveal two thin rows of even teeth. A weapon vaguely resembling a pistol hung from its belt.

'I'm looking for handbags.' Brodie recovered quickly. 'Which floor is that?'

She didn't wait for a reply. The creature reached for its weapon as she leapt into action. Brodie aimed a kick directly at its groin—she assumed its physiology was similar to that of a human—and followed up with three rapid punches to its jaw.

The thing hit the back of the lift before slowly sliding to the floor.

'You're the ugliest modification I've ever seen,' Brodie said. 'You make Jabba the Hutt look good.'

She had to hurry now. Dragging the ugly brute

out of the elevator, she grabbed his sidearm and jumped into the recess. Her eyes searched the display. Once again, the symbols were unfamiliar, but it was easy enough to ascertain the button for the top floor. She stabbed the control. As the elevator zoomed up through the ship at an amazing speed, she checked the gun. The barrel of it ended in a metallic grill; obviously this thing did not fire bullets. Apart from that, it was a simple enough weapon and seemed to have only one setting.

Shoot, Brodie thought. *That's easy enough.*

Her heart was thumping now. She had the element of surprise on her side, but not much else. This was not going to be easy.

The elevator doors whizzed open.

Brodie realized two things at once. One was that she had successfully reached the bridge of the ship—she could see a massive row of windows. Through them she could see that night had fallen and an ocean of stars filled the glass.

This detail fell to insignificance, however, as she realized the command center was being run by twenty creatures similar to the one she had just dispatched several floors below. She stood staring at the bizarre-looking creatures for all of five seconds before realizing that going down to another floor would be a good choice.

Except at that moment an alarm sounded—a long peal of doom that made every fishhead look up at each other. One of them happened to glance sideways at the open doors of the elevator.

'Nuts,' Brodie said.

She started forward, firing wildly and taking down eight of the creatures in a matter of seconds. At that point one of them fired back, stunning her, and she dropped the gun. Taking a woozy step forward, she shook her head to clear it, slammed her fist into the stomach of one of the nearby creatures and lifted it into the air.

The unfortunate victim then became a live battering ram as Brodie used it as both a weapon and a shield, smashing several of the other creatures to the ground while deflecting shots with its body. She had successfully taken down fifteen of the monsters before one of them came up behind her and stunned her a second time.

She sank to her knees, dropping her living shield headfirst into the floor. It was only when she was picked up that she looked through half open eyes to see the scene outside the window. It was crisply black, blacker than any night sky seen from Earth.

That's when the planet rolled into view. She saw the thin layer of atmosphere, an enormous expanse of ocean, layers of cloud and the East Coast of North America.

I am on a ship, Brodie thought. *A spaceship.*

Then everything went black around her.

Chapter Five

I arrived at the warehouse with five minutes to spare. By then I felt so stressed that the back of my head was throbbing with tension. The Agency forbade us from using our powers for anything other than Agency business, but this time I was prepared to make an exception. I had flown around the outskirts of the city before landing behind a warehouse in a rundown section of town where Las Vegas crumbled into desert.

This was the part of town that tourists didn't get to see. Abandoned buildings fighting a losing battle against nature. Decaying roads in need of repair. Even the homeless didn't come to this part of town; there was no-one to panhandle from and there was nowhere to buy food anyway.

I had done my best to stay focused on how to handle this situation, but by the time I landed I realized I'd barely moved forward an inch in my plans. There was one all-consuming thought that had taken over my brain.

They had Brodie.

They had kidnapped my girlfriend.

I felt as helpless as anyone else who has ever been blackmailed by a kidnapper. My powers had not given me an advantage; at least, not yet anyway. The short message sent on my phone was succinct and straight to the point: the kidnappers would kill Brodie if I did not follow their instructions; I was not to tell another living being about her kidnapping. Not anyone at The Agency. Not the police. Not any of my friends.

I was alone.

Looking out at the desert, I saw the never-ending horizon stretching away into the distance. The warehouse was surrounded by a wire fence. There was no sign of cars or other vehicles. No tracks in the sand. The building was little more than a huge sheet metal shed. It looked like one big wind might knock it down completely. The front door was slightly ajar. As I slowly walked towards it, I threw up a barrier around myself. At least if anyone attacked me, I would be prepared.

Easing myself through the gap in the door, I

found the interior to be dry and dusty. A timber mezzanine level ran around the top floor of the building. Old wooden boxes lay everywhere on the ground floor, but they all appeared to be overturned and empty. It was impossible to see what lay behind the boxes on the upper level.

Here goes nothing, I thought.

I stepped into the building, keeping my eyes trained on the mezzanine at all times. If anyone was up there, they—

A thing stepped out from behind one of the piles of boxes.

I say *thing* because it was not human. It was either an alien or a seriously enhanced mod. Enhanced humans were no surprise to me. I had encountered several of them already, although this thing looked radically different. It was tall, covered in scales and had a head not unlike a fish. A weapon's holster hung from its waist, but its gun was firmly planted in its hand. This was the last thing I expected, although when I thought about it I realized that Brodie would never be brought down by a regular kidnapper.

'Where's Brodie?' I asked.

'I am Graal,' the creature said. 'I am from a planet many light years from here. A planet called Tagaar. And I am disappointed. I had hoped you would attack me on sight.'

So I obliged him.

Lifting my arm, I used a ball of air to knock the gun from his hand. Then I dragged him down off the floor above and crashed him into the ground. Racing over to him, I slipped an arm around his neck as he started to rise. He looked momentarily dazed, but responded by flipping me over into a pile of boxes.

To really rile me up, he slowly rose to his feet and laughed.

I got ready to throw a hurricane at him.

'That would not be advisable,' he said. 'You have proven my point. You humans are a warlike race. You relish in your bloodshed. Your whole history is made up of killing those who are weaker.'

I was not interested in defending the history

of the human race. 'Where's Brodie?'

'She is safe.' Graal tilted his head and regarded me through one eye. 'For now. If you want her to remain uninjured you will follow my instructions exactly.'

As I looked at him I realized his lips were not matching his words exactly. They seemed to be out of sync.

'You are a primitive people,' he said. 'Of course, I am using a translator to communicate with you. My species was spanning the stars while you were still living in caves and eating raw meat.'

I decided to challenge him. 'Why are you kidnapping an innocent girl if you're so advanced?'

'I have my reasons.'

I felt like beating him to death so I could find out those reasons. He lifted his head and laughed again.

'Good. I see your anger,' he said. 'I like rage in a species.'

'I want evidence that Brodie is still alive.'

'I will not give it to you.'

I took a single step towards him and heard the sound of muffled feet from above. Glancing up, I saw a dozen similarly dressed aliens step out from behind boxes with their guns trained on me.

The headache in the back of my head switched to full gear as I felt the urge to tear Graal into pieces.

'What do you want?' I asked.

'I wish you to run an errand for me.' He paused. 'There is a vault deep within The Agency building where you are housed.'

'So?'

'A weapon is located in that vault. It was developed by the country known on your planet as China. I want that weapon stolen and delivered to me.'

'The Agency is built like an underground fortress,' I said. 'How am I supposed to break into the vault?'

'I have instructions on how to reach it. You will use your powers to steal the weapon.'

'What does it do?'

A smile played across the alien's lips. 'It is

most ingenious. It is a type of gun called the Stonekiller. It converts its victim into a type of living rock. They are unable to move a muscle, yet they remain alive, locked within the rock for all time.'

I tried to imagine such a fate. 'That's sick.'

'It is creative,' Graal laughed. 'Even my own people have not developed such a weapon. Only a perverse and violent species such as you humans could develop a torture so terrible.'

'We are not all like that,' I said. 'Most people want to live in peace.'

Graal shook his head. 'You misunderstand me, boy. I praise the savagery of your species. The Tagaar are a warrior race. We have driven more species to extinction than you can imagine.'

Great. Another unwanted history lesson.

'I want proof that Brodie is still alive.'

'You will simply have to take my word for that.'

'Why should I trust you?'

'Because you have no other choice.' He tapped a patch on his wrist and a holographic map appeared in the air before me. I recognized it immediately. It was a three-dimensional schema of The Agency. How they had acquired a map of the secret organization was anyone's guess.

'I will show you how to retrieve the Stonekiller,' Graal said. 'When you have delivered it to me, I will talk to you about saving the woman you love.'

Chapter Six

'Boys?' Ebony asked. 'Have you seen Axel?'

Dan and Chad looked up at her from their respective positions in the games room. Chad was doing bench presses. Dan was in the middle of a computer game called Burning Swords.

'No.' Dan did not look up from his game.

'Uh-uh.' Chad continued to push the weights up into the air.

'Fine.' She glared at both of them. 'It'll have to be you two then.'

'Us two…what?' Dan asked. He was at level seventy-two in the game and so far had been defeated by a three-headed, six-armed medieval warrior no fewer than fifteen times. He felt certain that if he—

Ebony folded her arms. 'We're going to spend some time with Ferdy.'

'We already spent some time with Ferdy.' Chad continued to work out with the barbell. 'We sent Mr. Robot Man to jail and made the world a better place. Don't you remember, sis?'

'I remember.' Ebony pursed her lips. 'I also

remember that you boys have hardly spent any time at all with Ferdy over the last week.'

'That's not true.' Chad rested the weight on the support bar. He slipped his shirt on. 'I've spent plenty of time with Ferdy.'

'Really? When?'

'Oh...' He thought for a moment. 'Oh, just lots of time.'

'Ferdy needs us,' Ebony said. 'He needs human contact.'

Dan sat down his computer game. The medieval warrior had defeated him for the sixteenth time. 'Come on, Ebony. We give him lots of attention. He's like a brother to us.'

'You certainly don't act like he's a brother.'

'Maybe a cousin.'

'Whatever.'

'He acts like we're in the way,' Chad said. 'He seems to like the computer more than he likes me.'

'A lot of people probably feel that way.' The sarcasm was lost on Chad. 'Ferdy needs people. He needs us.' She paused. 'Whether he knows it or not.'

'Sis…' Chad made one last feeble attempt.

'We're a family,' she said. 'Come on.'

She waited until she knew the boys were following her, then started down the corridor to Ferdy's room. The Agency had given him his own private chambers in the middle of one of the floors of the hotel. It had no windows, a feature that Ebony had opposed, but she could understand the logic of it.

It wasn't that The Agency considered Ferdy dangerous, but Agent Palmer had pointed out to them that Ferdy sometimes didn't know his own strength. He could lift a car and throw it fifty feet with little effort. What if he suddenly got it into his head to pick up a computer and hurl it at a passing vehicle?

Ebony was determined to make Ferdy feel wanted. It was the only way to bring him out of his autistic shell. She knocked at his door.

No answer.

She knocked again.

'Ferdy!' she called. 'Are you in there?'

'Ferdy is playing chess,' his voice replied.

'Can we come in?'

'Chess originated in India in the sixth century!'

'That's great, Ferdy. Can we come in?'

There was a long pause and then the door inched open. His face appeared in the gap.

'You are Ferdy's friends,' he said. 'Ferdy is playing chess.'

'Can we come in?' Chad asked. 'We thought we might hang out.'

'Spend some time together,' Dan said.

'Time is relative,' Ferdy said. 'Technically it is time/space.'

The three of them looked at each other before returning their gaze to Ferdy. They tried to look friendly.

'Come in,' Ferdy said.

They entered his room. Ebony glanced around. His quarters had changed little since they had arrived at The Agency. He had little in the way of possessions—not that any of them did—but his room looked more Spartan than their own. The few possessions he had acquired were neatly placed on shelves. A dozen computer monitors lined the walls. A chess set sat on the table in the middle of the room.

'You're very tidy,' Dan said. 'You can come and tidy our room if you like.'

'Ferdy cannot do the impossible,' Ferdy said.

'Oh,' Dan said. 'Look, I was—'

'Ferdy is joking,' he said. 'Ferdy was making a funny joke with his friends.'

Chad's eyes settled on the chess set. 'Who were you playing against?'

'The computer,' Ferdy said. 'Ferdy is playing one hundred and seven games.'

Ebony thought she had misheard him. 'You mean you've played a hundred and seven games against the computer?'

'No. Ferdy has played nine thousand, seven hundred and forty-one games since coming to live at the Las Vegas branch of The Agency.' He went over to a control panel and the dozen monitors sprang to life. They showed a multitude of chess games in various stages of play. 'Ferdy is concurrently playing one hundred and seven games against The Agency computer.'

'Concurrently?' Dan said.

'At the same time?' Chad said.

'That is the meaning of concurrent,' Ferdy said. 'Ferdy likes to play chess.'

'Are you winning many?' Chad asked.

He looked at Chad as if he had said something strange. 'Ferdy always wins.'

'Always?' Dan laughed.

'Always is a period of time without barriers, but traditionally understood to continue into the future,' Ferdy explained. 'There have also been more than twelve musical albums entitled Always as well as over thirty individual songs with the same name. In addition—'

'Uh, we get the idea,' Ebony said. 'We were thinking about going up to the roof to play ball.'

'Ball?'

'Yeah, you know, Ferdy,' Chad said. 'A spherical object typically made of—'

'Chad!' Ebony snapped.

'We're going to throw a ball around,' Chad said.

'Around what?'

'To each other,' Ebony explained. 'We'll throw it to each other. You know, for fun.'

'Ferdy finds this difficult to understand,' he said. 'If each of us wants a ball, then we should just all go and purchase our own balls.'

Dan shook his head. 'You could destroy the world of football with that kind of thinking.'

Ebony ignored him. 'Let's go.'

They found an elevator and ascended to the roof, stepping out into the light of a bright afternoon. The Agency owned the entire building, but most of it was still restricted. Fortunately the roof had been left to them, probably because a high wall ran around the exterior, shielding them from the outside world.

'I'm going to throw the ball to Chad,' Ebony said. 'Then he will throw it to Dan and he will throw it to you.'

Ebony threw the ball and each of them passed it to each other. When it reached Ferdy, he caught it and stood looking at it. Ebony realized she had left out an important detail.

'Now you throw it to Chad,' she said.

Ferdy threw it. Chad caught it and the game continued. After the ball had done the rounds a few more times, Dan went to catch it, but he winced in sudden pain.

The others hurried over to him.

'What is it, buddy?' Chad asked.

'It's my head,' he explained. 'I'm getting images. It's Brodie…'

'What is it?' Ebony asked. 'Is she okay?'

'No. I can sense desperation…pain…'

'Has she been in an accident?' Chad asked.

'No…I don't know…I'm not sure…'

Chad produced his cell phone. 'I'll try ringing her.' After a minute, he shook his head. 'No answer.'

'She's been gone all afternoon,' Ebony said.

'I thought it was weird when she didn't pick up earlier,' Chad said. 'Maybe she's in trouble.'

'I think we should speak to Agent Palmer,' Ebony said.

Ferdy picked up the ball. 'Ferdy throw the ball.'

'Okay, Ferdy,' Ebony said absently. 'But we've got to go inside.'

Ferdy drew his arm back and threw it hard into the air. They watched as it soared over the wall, across rooftops and past buildings into the sky. It finally disappeared into the distance, a tiny black dot racing towards the far horizon.

'Ferdy has friends,' the boy said. 'And he knows how to throw the ball.'

'Right on both counts,' Chad said.

Chapter Seven

Brodie awoke to find herself being dragged behind something that looked like it had escaped from a horror film. It wasn't one of the creatures that she had fought on the flight deck of the spaceship. It was larger, covered in shaggy hair, and made a strange grunting sound as it moved.

She lifted her head slightly.

'Hey, ugly,' she called.

The creature stopped and turned its head. Its face was a cross between a gorilla and a bear. Saliva dripped from its open mouth onto its hairy chest.

'I was right,' Brodie said. 'You are ugly.'

With her free leg, Brodie kicked the thing in the back of the leg as hard as possible. Through luck more than skill, she must have hit a pressure point because the creature immediately released her and fell backward.

Brodie rolled out of the way before it could land on her. As it hit the deck, she leapt up and directed a kick at the creature's throat. It let out an inarticulate gasp of pain. Running down the corridor as fast as she could, she had almost reached the end before she heard the burst of weapon fire behind her. A shock like a bolt of electricity ran through her body and darkness swallowed her again.

When she next awoke she found herself in another cell. The difference this time was that she was sharing this cell with other beings. She sat up and looked at them blearily. She had been stunned three times now and her body was beginning to feel as if a tractor had run over her.

'Who are you people?' she asked. 'What the hell is going on?'

'We are many,' one of them said cryptically. 'My name is Zena. I am from Corrida. They are from other worlds.' Zena was a woman with a catlike face; a fine coating of red hair covered it. She pointed to the other two occupants of the cell; a lizard woman and a short gray faced man who lay asleep on the floor. 'That is Bax, a woman from Frakaal. The sleeping man is Sadara from Forbus Nine.'

Now Brodie understand the meaning of the girl's words. 'You are many. You mean you are from many worlds. What are you doing here?'

'We are here to fight,' Bax said. 'To fight and to die.'

What a bright and positive environment, Brodie thought.

'Fight?' she said. 'Do you mean each other or—'

'The Tagaar,' Zena said. 'They are the aliens who kidnapped you. They are a warrior species that loves to fight and kill.'

Brodie frowned. 'They've come a long way to fight and kill me.'

'Their goal is larger than you,' Bax said. 'It is your planet.'

'What?'

'The Tagaar are excluded from the Union of Planets because of their warlike ways. They actively work to keep planets from joining the Union by promoting war and disharmony. Eventually they present themselves to one of the warring sides as a savior and offer to supply weapons and technology.'

Zena continued. 'After a time they begin to

install troops and military bases under the guise of co-operation and friendship.' She snorted. 'Then the killings begin. The assassinations. The terrorist attacks. By the time the species realize what is happening, it is too late. The Tagaar have become the masters of their planet.'

'How do you know all this?' Brodie asked.

'Because it happened to our worlds,' Zena said. 'Corrida was once a beautiful place, but our people did not treat our world with respect. We were in a state of constant war. Then the Tagaar appeared and sided with one of the superpower nations. Within months a world war had broken out. By the time it was all over, the Tagaar were the only ones standing.'

Bax nodded. 'It was a similar story on my world.'

'So what are you doing here?' Brodie asked.

'The Tagaar like to fight,' Zena said. 'They pick the best warriors from a world and fight against them.' The woman looked at Brodie. 'You must be a great fighter, otherwise you would not be here.'

Wonderful, Brodie thought. *If only I were a*

housewife in Sydney...

'I'm a mod,' Brodie said. She went on to explain modifications and how the Earth had changed over the last few months.

'Your planet must be growing close to joining the Union,' Zena said.

'I suppose so,' Brodie said.

'You will prove a worthy adversary for the Tagaar,' Bax said. 'That is good. It will keep you alive for longer.'

Brodie did not reply. She was thinking about the Earth and how little respect people had for it. The Tagaar must have rubbed their hands together with glee when they realized how much disunity already existed on the planet; war, religious conflict, terrorism, overpopulation, global warming. The list went on. It was amazing humanity hadn't wiped itself out already.

There's always hope, Brodie thought. *We still have friendship. Love. Co-operation. We're not all bad.*

A sound came from the corridor outside the

chamber. They all looked up. Brodie caught a glimpse of fear in Zena and Bax's eyes. Even the man who had been asleep—Sadara—sat up and stared at the door.

It opened and three of the Tagaar appeared. One of them was obviously their leader. He wore a fur around his shoulders with epaulets. His eyes settled on Brodie.

'Ah, here is the troublesome human,' he said.

Brodie said nothing.

'I am Breel,' he said. 'I am the commander of this vessel. I congratulate you on the way you fought on the bridge. You killed two of my men, including my chief navigator.'

'I'm sorry,' Brodie said. 'I don't like to kill anyone.'

'He was a terrible navigator. I have already replaced him.'

'Why am I here?' Brodie asked. 'I demand you release me at once.'

Breel smirked. 'I like that. Courage and bravery are good traits to have. Perhaps your species is not as worthless as I was led to believe.'

'We will fight you!' Brodie clenched her teeth. 'We will defeat you!'

'You may fight us, but you will not win.' Breel looked at her thoughtfully for a moment. 'You are here because we want you to fight, but we are also holding you as a hostage so that your mate will do our bidding.'

It took Brodie a moment to digest this information. 'Axel? Do your bidding?'

'If that is his name,' Breel said. 'One of our men is using him to cause disharmony on your world.'

'He won't follow your orders.'

'He already is. It is surprising what a man will do for a woman he loves.'

Brodie was stuck for an answer. 'When will I be released?'

Breel laughed. 'When we are finished with you.' The alien swung his head about. 'You. It is your time to fight again.'

He was looking directly at Sadara. The man

slowly stood and looked to the three of them in the cell. 'If I die,' he said, 'I go to the afterlife, to S'billa. My wife and children await me there.'

Brodie stared at him in horror. 'Your arm—'

He looked down at it. 'Broken in the last fight,' he explained. 'I have nothing to fear. I am ready to go to the land of my ancestors.'

'No!' Brodie leapt to her feet. 'This is wrong! It's inhuman! You can't expect this man to fight. He's injured!'

'It is inhuman,' Breel said. 'But we are not human. We are Tagaar.'

'No!' Brodie yelled.

The two guards grabbed her and held her back as Sadara walked from the room. Just before he left, the grey-faced alien looked back at Brodie.

'Save your strength, little one,' he said. 'You will need it for later.'

The guards threw Brodie to the floor. Brodie lay there in horror as the door closed shut.

'Sadara was right,' Bax said. 'Save your strength. In a few hours you will be fighting for your life.'

Chapter Eight

'Axel!'

I was halfway across The Hub when the voice came from behind me.

Damn. It was Chad and the others. They hurried over.

'Something's wrong with Brodie,' Chad said.

'What?' I looked at them in confusion. 'What do you mean?'

'Dan's getting one of those weird head things,' Ebony said. 'You know, like when he picks up people's thoughts.'

'So she's alive,' I said.

'Of course she's alive.' Chad looked at me strangely. 'But she must be in trouble. We're going to see Agent Palmer.'

'Okay,' I said. 'I'll see you there.'

'Where are you going?' Ebony asked.

'I have to wash up.'

'Wash up?' Chad said. 'But Brodie's in trouble!'

'Yeah.' I was not handling this very well. I

wanted to tell them the truth, but that would just get Brodie killed. 'I have to go to the toilet.'

'Whatever.' Ebony shook her head. 'We'll see you at Palmer's office.'

'Sure.'

I watched them go. Chad cast a long last look over his shoulder at me. He looked furious. I didn't blame him.

Waiting till they were out of sight, I crossed to the opposite side of the concourse where a bank of elevators were located. I had never used these before; I had never had any reason to do so. Punching a button, I waited a few seconds before one arrived and I stepped inside.

My heart was thumping. I pulled out a security pass. It had been supplied to me by Graal. How he had acquired it was a mystery, but now I swiped it across the reader and hit the button for Sub-Level Thirty. At the last moment a security guard stepped into the elevator with me. Staring straight ahead, I ignored him as we descended to my level. I climbed out and walked straight ahead until the doors closed behind me.

Then I let out a breath and sagged against a wall. I wasn't cut out to be a spy. I checked the device attached to my wrist. It was a three-dimensional compass with a map of the area. Another gift from Graal. The device indicated a supply room on my left. I hurried down the corridor, found the room and stepped inside.

Closing the door behind me, I expected to hear alarms explode all over the complex and security guards to appear from nowhere. Instead, the only sound was the buzz of the air conditioning and the thudding of my own heart.

This is completely wrong, I thought. *I should go upstairs and speak to Agent Palmer and tell her what's going on.*

Except if I did that, Brodie might die, and I was not prepared to let that happen. My brief conversation with the others had already confirmed she was still alive. Involving The Agency would only endanger her life. I had to do this. Alone. Later, when Brodie was safe, I would make things right.

I hoped.

An air conditioning grill was set into the wall above one of the storage racks. I wrenched it free, stepped up onto one of the racks and climbed in. Again I expected a dozen alarms to explode into action, but nothing happened. I slid down the access shaft until I reached a junction. It was dark, so I produced my cell phone and activated the torch. Taking a turn to the right, I followed it for about a hundred feet until I reached another turn. I followed this until I reached the end.

This next step would be impossible for anyone else because before me lay a slim shaft that went into a straight drop for hundreds of feet. I was unsure exactly how far; the map did not indicate the distance. I slid over the edge and slowly lowered myself into the shaft. Finally I used my powers to lower myself downward.

I would be finished if my powers failed now. I would fall for an eternity before smashing headfirst into the floor far below.

I tried to imagine what the others would make

of my absence.

Both Brodie and Axel are gone…

They must have eloped…

Sir, we're getting a very strange smell from ventilation shaft P18…

I continued downward. After the first hundred feet I began to really wonder about the depth of this shaft. What if it continued for miles? What if my concentration wandered? What if a security system existed within the shaft that—

A bend in the shaft appeared before me. Letting out a long breath, I slowly lowered myself to the floor below. I curled up and lay gasping in fetal position. Sweat was running down my back. A crick of pain had opened up on the right hand side of my neck under my jaw. I felt like a nervous wreck. Was I too young to have a heart attack?

How was I going to survive this?

Because I had no other choice.

Because Brodie was depending on me.

The shaft opened out into a wider, flatter rectangular prism. I slid along it towards a metal grate about fifty feet in front of me. A slight breeze moved against my face. Finally I reached the grate and pressed my face against it. I saw a thin, rectangular chamber beyond with an elevator to one side.

'Oh hell,' I said.

A round door the size of a fully grown man was set into the opposite wall. It had a digital combination lock on the front. Fortunately, Graal had supplied me with the code to open the door. At least I knew I could get in. That wasn't the issue.

I peered upward through the holes of the grill. The real issue lay directly above my position because a security camera sat a foot above my head. It was focused on the door of the safe. There was no doubt in my mind that alarm bells would start ringing if I turned the camera off or tried to reposition it.

I was stuck.

Chapter Nine

Dan's head felt like it was about to explode.

The pain began at the back of his skull and vibrated all the way across the top to a point between his eyes. One of the trainers at The Agency had called this his Third Eye, a point of psychic ability within Eastern mysticism. Dan had another name for it.

Frikkin painful!

He looked across at the others. Chad and Ferdy were seated opposite him in the waiting area directly outside Agent Palmer's office. Ebony was sitting next to him with a sympathetic hand on his shoulder. A secretary sat outside Agent Palmer's office. She was an older woman with a severe expression. She had already shot them several disapproving looks.

Dan glanced at Ebony. He liked the quiet girl. Not only was she always friendly towards him, but she didn't treat him like a baby.

Unlike her brother.

Chad stuck out his jaw. 'Suck it up, little man. You gotta be tough to be a superhero.'

Little man?

'Get lost.'

Chad cast his eyes to the ceiling. 'I'm just saying you gotta have a backbone if you want—'

'Backbone?' Dan felt the heat rising to his face. 'My head feels like it's about to explode!'

'It can't be that bad!' Chad said. 'If you can't handle the heat—'

That was enough for Dan. Fortunately, Chad was sitting on a metal chair which made it all the easier to lift it—and him—straight up off the ground.

'Hey! What—'

'Get some backbone!' Dan yelled as Chad crashed headfirst into the drywall ceiling. 'Suck it up!'

A ball of flame burst from Chad's hand and flew towards Dan. The younger boy dove to one side as the fireball hit his chair and sent it flying. The secretary screamed and dove under her desk. Ebony shrieked and leapt in the opposite direction. Chad and the chair hit the ground in an untidy pile. He swore and started to his feet. Only Ferdy remained seated.

His eyes were focused on the new hole in the ceiling.

'Abraham Lincoln was the sixteenth President of the United States,' Ferdy told them. 'Born in—'

'Fire alert,' a computerized voice intoned from a speaker set into the ceiling. 'Fire alert. Warning. Fire alert.'

The door to Agent Palmer's office burst open. 'What on Earth is going on out here?'

'They're out of control!' Only the top of the secretary's head showed above her desk. 'They're running amuck!'

'Is that true?' Palmer asked.

'Only a little amuck.' Ebony climbed to her feet. 'We need to see you for a few minutes.'

'It's important,' Dan said.

Palmer studied the chaotic scene. 'All right. Five minutes. No more. I've got paperwork coming out of my ears.'

They followed her into the office and sat down.

'It's about Brodie,' Dan and Ebony started together.

They stopped.

Ebony continued. She explained about Dan's headache and that they had not seen Brodie all day. Agent Palmer interlocked her fingers and listened in silence until she finished. Then she started punching keys on her computer.

'We should be able to get an idea of her location within seconds,' the agent said. 'We can trace the phones through their SIM cards.'

'You can trace our calls?' Chad did not look pleased.

'No,' Palmer said. 'Not your calls. Just the phones. We can locate the phone by triangulating its position off cell towers.' She punched a few more keys and waited. 'This should only take a few seconds.'

They waited while the agent stared at the screen.

'That's odd,' Agent Palmer finally said.

'What is?' Chad asked.

'I'm not getting anything.'

'Maybe the phone's switched off.'

'We should still be getting a signal.' The agent drummed her fingers on the desk. 'That makes no sense.'

'Why is there no signal?' Ebony asked.

'I can only think of a few possible reasons,' Palmer said. 'Possibly the phone has been destroyed.'

'Destroyed?' Dan didn't like the sound of that. 'How would that happen?'

'There are other possibilities,' Agent Palmer said. 'The phone could simply be out of range. It might be too far underground for us to trace, or maybe it has developed a fault we're not familiar with.'

Dan realized his headache had dissipated. He was relieved it was gone, but now he began to worry that it might have a more tragic implication.

'You don't think Brodie's dead—do you?'

'Let's not jump to conclusions here. How long has she been gone?'

'Since this morning.'

'Even local law enforcement wouldn't do anything until she's been gone twenty-four hours,' she said. 'Let's give her till tonight.'

'And then what?' Ebony asked.

'Then we'll start a search for her.'

Chad frowned. 'How?'

'How what?'

'The Agency is a secret organisation,' Chad said. 'You're hardly going to contact the police. Are you?'

Agent Palmer shrugged. 'This is all hypothetical. Right now—'

'It might not be hypothetical in a few hours' time,' Chad said. 'How are you going to explain to the police that Brodie is living here? That she's part of The Agency?'

'I know you're upset—'

'Just answer my questions.'

The silence hung between them like a curtain.

'All right.' The agent looked uncomfortable. 'You might as well know that The Agency has been liaising with the US government since the United Nations revealed mods to the world. We have established a memorandum of understanding between us.'

'What does that mean?' Dan asked.

'A deal.' Chad glared at the agent. 'Nice of you to tell us.'

'We don't have to tell you anything.'

'Like hell,' Chad said. 'My sister and I aren't even US citizens. We're Norwegian. We can leave at any time.'

'I wouldn't advise it.'

Chad looked like he was about to explode so Ebony grabbed his arm.

'We're all a little wound up, right now,' she said. 'We're worried about Brodie. Let's just deal with one thing at a time.'

Chad didn't say anything, but he nodded.

'I'll keep on trying her phone during the afternoon,' Palmer said. 'We'll call in reinforcements if she doesn't turn up by tonight.'

The group silently marched out of her office. The secretary at the desk outside gave them a severe look, but they ignored her. Ferdy drew close to Ebony as they walked down the corridor.

'Brodie is missing,' he said.

'That's right. Brodie is missing.'

'She is Ferdy's friend.'

'She's a friend to all of—' Ebony stopped. 'Wait a minute.'

The others looked at her.

'Where the hell is Axel?'

Chapter Ten

It's a good thing cell phones are so versatile these days, I thought. *This would have been impossible ten years ago.*

Dislodging the grill from the air vent, I pulled it into the cramped space next to me. Using my powers, I levitated the cell phone so it hovered only a few inches below the camera. I used it to take a picture of the room. The next step was the most dangerous. Keeping the phone just below the camera, I focused on the light illuminating the room. Fortunately it was a simple fluorescent tube set into the ceiling. By compressing the air at one end of the light, I was able to break the contact, causing the light to flicker.

In that brief instant, I levitated the phone upward before the camera. Even if someone was watching the camera, they would probably assume the light was starting to fail. Hence the flicker. Hopefully they would fail to realize they were now looking at a photo of the room instead of the room itself.

Sliding out of the ventilation shaft, I dropped

down to the floor below. I had to remain focused on keeping the phone completely stationery before the camera. This was difficult, but not impossible; The Agency had trained me well over the last few months. I crossed quickly to the enormous door, examined the keypad and inserted the code.

Bingo!

I heard the clunk of metal rods sliding back into place as the lock disengaged. I opened the door.

Now for the Stonekiller.

The room was lined with shelving on each side. I felt a tinge of guilt at my betrayal. Stealing other people's possessions was not something I had ever engaged in, but it had to be done. Keeping an eye on my phone suspended before the camera, I quickly scanned the shelves. Graal had shown me a picture of the gun. The device was similar in shape to a normal handgun, but the body and barrel were about three times the size. There were several objects lining the shelves. Nothing looked like the Stonekiller.

I felt a rising sense of panic. What if the weapon wasn't here? What if it lay in some other vault of The Agency? What if I had to return to Graal empty-handed?

A sound came from the outside chamber. Glancing through the door, I saw nothing. The elevator doors remained closed. I was imagining things.

A new thought struck me as I returned my attention to the shelves; the gun was probably not sitting by itself on one of the shelves. It was probably enclosed in a container. On a shelf second from the bottom lay a small, gray carry case with a molded handle.

Opening it, I found the gun inside. It looked terribly innocent when I considered the terrible power it contained.

They are unable to move a muscle, yet they remain alive, locked within the rock for all time…

How terrible. I tried not to think of the repercussions of handing this weapon over to Graal, but I could not allow Brodie to be harmed. Once she was safe, I would retrieve the weapon and then—

Another sound seemed to come from the

chamber outside the vault. I stepped towards the open door, but at the same time caught a glimpse of a flashing light above the doorway of the vault. I had not seen it when I entered the room as it was above my head, but now I stared at it in absolute horror.

A camera lay above the door and it was trained directly on me.

I swore.

Another sound came from the chamber outside, but this time I recognized it. The elevator was descending. I bolted from the chamber with the case in my hand. My attention left my cell phone completely. It crashed to the floor as the doors of the elevator slid open. Four security guards with rifles burst through. Their guns narrowed on me.

'Drop the case!' one of them screamed. 'Lay down on the floor—'

Sorry. Not today.

I threw up a shield and ran straight at them. They fired. Bullets ricocheted. I leapt into the air. Dove over them straight into the elevator. Spinning about, I slammed the button for the top floor. The men spun about. Fired again. Several of the bullets hit my shield. Crashed into the walls of the elevator. The doors slid shut.

Falling back into the wall of the elevator, I felt my heart beating crazily in my chest. I felt light-headed. The Agency knew about me now. They knew I had the Stonekiller. Nothing would ever be the same again.

The elevator shuddered to a halt. The lights dimmed. I focused on the ceiling and smashed it into pieces. I flew upward through the debris. An alarm began to ring. I rose up about a hundred feet. Reached a pair of elevator doors. Wrenched them open with my mind.

The passageway beyond had a pair of scientists walking down it straight towards me. I flew at them. They dove to the floor. I had no idea what level I was on. I just had to find a way out of here. A sign whizzed past me. B12. I was still twelve levels down. Damn. This wasn't going to be easy.

An elevator shaft lay at the far end of the corridor. I didn't bother waiting for a ride. Possibly all the elevators were stopped now anyway. I forced the doors open. Stepped into the shaft. Flew straight up. An elevator was heading straight down towards me.

'Sorry,' I said.

I slammed into the bottom of the elevator. Pushed it upward until I reached the top of the shaft. Another pair of doors lay before me. I took a deep breath. Focused on the doors. Forced them open. Twenty armed guards with rifles surrounded the doors in a tight semi-circle. They opened fire. I started forward, releasing the elevator behind me. Bullets slammed into my shield. I flinched. Fell back. Pushed my way through the barrage. One of the guards started forward and I used my mind to pick him up and throw him towards the center of the squad. They fell about in a heap as the firing continued. It was a deafening roar. I leapt into the air above them. I had reached the concourse. Now I needed the street.

I could try going up another elevator shaft, but bursting out of a hotel in the middle of Las Vegas would leave The Agency completely exposed. I could not do that. A better option was the exit shafts that led to the desert. I streaked through the air across The Hub, found one of the tunnels and zoomed down it.

It was all completely surreal. Only a few hours before I had returned from a mission as part of a team. Now I was leaving all that behind. How could I ever be part of The Agency again?

'Hey!'

The voice came from behind me. I recognized it immediately—and ignored it. Within seconds I reached the outer doors of the tunnel. Forcing them open, I flew out into the warm air of the desert.

The cry came from behind me again. I turned to see Chad about fifty feet behind me riding on a surfboard of fire. It was a technique he had been trying to perfect for weeks. More often than not, he had fallen straight out of the sky.

'What the hell are you doing?' he screamed.

I looked at him in dismay as I flew backward across the desert. I struggled to speak.

'I can't tell you!' I yelled. 'You have to leave

me alone.'

'I can't do that.'

'You've got to!'

He drew his arm back to create a ball of fire, but I was faster. In an instant, I built up a gust of air and threw it at him. He fell sideways off his fiery surfboard and plummeted downward. Just before he hit the ground, I used my powers to soften the impact.

He did not move.

What had I done?

There was no time to find an answer to that terrible question, so I turned and flew away.

Chapter Eleven

'This is outrageous!' Agent Palmer slammed her fist into the table. 'I demand an explanation!'

Ebony was sitting in Agent Palmer's office in the same seat she had occupied only a few short hours before. She stared helplessly at the other members of the team. There weren't many other eyes that stared back. Brodie was still missing. Axel was gone. Chad had chased after him and now he had also disappeared. All that remained was herself, Dan and Ferdy. Dan looked completely bewildered. Ferdy calmly met her gaze before looking up at Agent Palmer.

'The domain extension for websites in Romania is dot RO,' he said.

Palmer's face went a brighter shade of red. She had been standing, but now she collapsed back into her seat and didn't speak for a long time. It occurred to Ebony that she was probably counting to ten.

Finally the agent swallowed hard and leant forward. 'Let's go through what we know. When was the last time you saw Brodie? And Axel?'

Ebony went through the day's events again. There was little to add from what had been previously discussed. Brodie had been missing all day. Axel had completed the mission that morning. Palmer asked her a few questions.

'Did he seem strange?'

'Not at all,' Ebony said.

'How about nervous?'

'No.'

'Has he ever expressed any particular hatred for The Agency?'

No more than any of us, Ebony thought.

'No,' she said.

'Any strange calls?'

'No.'

'None?'

'Who would ring us?' Ebony asked. 'We only know each other.'

Dan spoke. 'This all started when Brodie went missing.'

Agent Palmer considered this. 'In that case,

her disappearance has escalated into something far bigger.'

'Like what?' Dan asked. 'What's going on?'

The agent seemed to consider her words carefully before continuing. 'Axel has broken into a vault below the complex and stolen a weapon. A very dangerous weapon. How he came to know of it is a mystery. What he intends to do with it is also a mystery.' She drummed her fingers on the desk. 'I can only assume that Axel has been turned.'

'Turned?' Ebony asked. 'Into what?'

She had images of him morphing into a bug.

'By a foreign power,' the agent said. 'He's a traitor.'

'That's ridiculous!' Ebony snapped.

'He would never do such a thing,' Dan said. 'He would never betray us.'

'But it appears he has.'

The voice came from behind them. A man stood in the doorway. It took Ebony a moment to recognize him. It was Twenty-Two.

Agent Palmer looked flustered. 'Twenty-Two.

I was about to file a report—'

He shook his hand. 'Don't worry about your reports, Agent Palmer. Matters would seem to be moving rather more quickly than that.' He regarded Ebony and the others with an even gaze. 'I think I would like to hear about the day's events from our young friends.'

For what now seemed like the hundredth time, Ebony related what had happened. The alien listened to her in silence.

'So it would seem that Brodie and Axel have betrayed us—'

'That would never happen!' Dan said.

'—or Axel is being blackmailed somehow,' Twenty-Two said.

'Blackmailed?' Ebony asked. 'With what?'

'With Brodie. She may have been kidnapped.'

Ebony let the idea sink in. She found it hard to imagine that Brodie could be kidnapped. She was so powerful, after all. Yet any of them could be overcome under the right circumstances.

'No matter what the situation,' the alien

continued, 'we must treat Axel as a hostile force.'

'Hostile?' Dan said.

'Until his loyalty can be verified,' Twenty-Two said, 'Axel must be treated as an enemy of The Agency.'

'That's not fair!' Ebony said.

'Life is often unfair,' the alien responded. 'I must ask you to remain in the compound until this situation is resolved.'

'But we haven't done anything!'

'You must remain here for your own protection.' Twenty-Two turned to Agent Palmer. 'Continue with your investigations. The Stonekiller must be recovered at all costs.' He gave everyone a final nod before leaving the room.

'What is the Stonekiller?' Ebony asked.

With a weary sigh, Agent Palmer described the weapon to them.

'Axel would have no reason to ever steal such a thing,' Dan said. 'And what would he do with it?'

'It's not what he would do with it,' Palmer said. 'It's what a foreign power would use it for.'

'But—' Ebony began.

The agent held up a hand. 'That's all for now. You are confined to the compound. Whether Axel and Brodie have turned or are acting under duress, we need to keep you under lock and key until this situation is resolved. Our security cameras show Chad was in pursuit of Axel. I assume he will be returning shortly. The same rules will apply to him.'

There seemed to be very little to say after that. Ebony led the others from the room. She remained silent until they reached the concourse.

'We're going to find Brodie and the others,' Ebony said.

'But Agent Palmer said—'

'Forget Agent Palmer! We're not trained sheep! It looks like Brodie's been kidnapped and Axel is trying to save her. And why hasn't Chad returned?'

'Chad often acts in a highly independent manner,' Ferdy said. 'Sometimes he is a painful individual.'

'He is still your friend.' Ebony laid a hand on

his arm. 'He still cares about you.'

'Ferdy knows this,' the boy acknowledged. 'We must help our friends.'

'Absolutely,' Ebony said. 'Now we just need to find a way out of here.'

Dan started. 'But Agent Palmer said—'

'We're going to escape from The Agency,' Ebony interrupted him. 'We're going to steal a Flex Fighter and fly it right out of here.'

Chapter Twelve

The last light of day creased the horizon as the Tagaar fighter ship slowly descended into the valley. The craft had been invisible during flight, but now the cloak was deactivated for landing. Dust and desert scrub were blown about by the exhaust of the ship as it settled onto the dry earth. Finally the rear of the vessel opened and Graal stepped down the ramp flanked by a team of warriors.

The Tagaar leader perused the landscape. They had sighted a long dirt road from the air and followed it to the abandoned shack with its leaning porch and broken windows. T'bar, his second in command, appeared at his side. They drew their weapons as they peered into the gloom.

'Is this the place?' T'bar looked about. 'There seems to be nothing here.'

'This is the right place.' Graal remained motionless as his men fanned out into the surrounding desert and circled the shack. 'A signal has been emanating from here for several days.'

'It cannot be an accident,' T'bar said.

'It is no accident.'

Graal shivered, not from fear, but from the cold. This air was too chilled for a Tagaar warrior! His people needed hot, steamy environments in which to flourish. The climate of this world was unnatural— it even had ice at its poles!

He knew the inhabitants were currently in the process of heating its atmosphere, but it couldn't happen fast enough as far as he was concerned. That process would accelerate once the planet had fallen under Tagaar control.

The sooner the better, he thought. *The empire must expand. An empire that does not grow is destined to die.*

'You've come a long way,' a voice called from the darkness.

His men opened fire.

A deafening roar filled the valley as laser blasts struck the shack. Within seconds the windows and walls were demolished and it was possible to see straight through the structure. Several more seconds passed as Graal screamed to make himself heard.

'I gave no order to fire!' he roared.

The weapons fire drew to an untidy halt as Graal strode down the ramp. The Tagaar were born and bred to fight. It had been their way of life for millennia. Unfortunately, it meant they sometimes shot first and asked questions later.

'We were called here for a reason,' he said. 'I wanted to discover that reason.'

'I'm pleased to hear that,' the voice spoke again.

Graal and his men looked warily about in confusion.

A woman appeared at Graal's side. She seemed to appear from thin air. His men raised their weapons, but then cried out in dismay. Graal looked at them in confusion. They were pointing their guns at their own heads.

What in Bruuk's name was going on?

'I have temporarily taken control of your men,' the woman said.

'Who are you?' Graal asked.

'I am Morgan Le Fay. I wish to speak to you

about the future of this planet.' She walked around him as if examining a sculpture. 'We both know that change is in the air.'

'What are you? Are you human?'

'What I am is unimportant,' she confirmed. 'You may think of me as a hunter; my fellow humans are the hunted.'

That was a concept Graal could appreciate.

Graal introduced himself. 'We are the Tagaar. We have come to this world—'

'I know why you have come to this world,' Morgan said. 'I have been aware of your species for centuries, as indeed I have known of the Union of Planets.'

'Then you know our intentions are peaceful.'

Morgan's laughter rang out long and high across the desert sands. Graal felt rage burning within him. He did not like to be laughed at—especially by a human. And a woman at that!

'Peaceful?' Morgan asked. 'You must think me a fool. The Tagaar are one of the most warlike races in the galaxy. I know your tactics of disruption and eventual colonization of worlds. I know your only desire is to conquer this planet.'

'You seem to know a great deal.' Graal cast his eyes across his men, who continued to hold their guns against their heads. 'I will ask you to release my men. They will not harm you.'

Morgan made a motion with her hand.

'Your men are free.'

The men lowered their weapons uncertainly.

'We received your signal—' Graal started.

'As I knew you would.'

'—and we have come to its source,' Graal said. 'What is it you desire?'

'What makes you think I desire anything?'

'Everyone desires something.' The desert was growing colder by the moment. 'Is it gold? Or gems? Or—'

'I do desire something,' Morgan said. 'I have lived a long time and I have seen a great many things.'

'And yet?'

'I have outgrown this world. The time has

come for me to leave.'

'I see.' Graal considered the woman's words. 'You need a ship.'

'A starship.' She gave him a broad smile. 'I like traveling. Visiting distant lands. Meeting new people. Consuming them.'

'Consuming—'

'Never mind.' The smile grew broader. 'Let's make a deal.'

'What do we get in return?'

'This planet.'

'We could conquer this planet if we wished,' Graal said. 'We have conquered many worlds. We have expanded our empire to make it the most powerful in the galaxy.'

'That's a lie and you know it,' Morgan said. 'The League is more powerful than you, but they are constrained by their own moral principles. They will attack you if you attack the Earth.'

'We are powerful—'

Morgan cut him off. 'You are powerful, but it is easier to be welcomed here as heroes than as enemies. You want this world in so much disarray that the human race will beg for your assistance.'

'And you can achieve this?'

'I can bring this planet to its knees. There will be widespread panic. Governments will collapse. You will arrive at the right time to come to its aid. The Tagaar will be welcomed as heroes.'

'How long will this take?'

'Only a matter of days.' She paused. 'But I will need a small component from one of your ships. A quantum resonator.'

'I am not familiar with that piece of equipment.'

She described it to him.

T'bar stirred at his side. 'I know the device to which she refers.'

Graal nodded. This campaign was estimated to take months. Now an opportunity had fallen into his lap to bring about the same result in a fraction of that time. And if this woman failed, he still had his other plan in motion.

And all of this for a starship, Graal thought.

That's a small price to pay for a world.

'Is it a deal?' Morgan asked.

The woman held out her hand. Graal stared at it blankly until he realized she wanted to link her hand with his own. He took her hand, expecting it to be warm. Much to his surprise, her skin was icy cold.

'It is a deal,' Graal said.

The night gathered around them.

Chapter Thirteen

'That's impossible,' Dan said. 'How are we going to steal a Flex Fighter?'

'Few things are impossible,' Ferdy said. 'Stealing a Flex may be difficult, but it is entirely possible.'

'And then what? We still need to find Brodie and the others.'

'You'll have to use your mind reading trick,' Ebony said. 'We'll use you like a human metal detector to track down Brodie and the others.'

'I'm not sure—'

'Well, I am,' Ebony interrupted. 'Come on.'

One of the many tunnels leading into the compound was a service tunnel filled with Flex aircraft. While they normally did not depart from here, Ebony had noticed the craft were usually parked here when not in use.

'This is a maintenance area,' Ferdy said.

The Flex vessels were in various states of repair. Men were working on a number of them. Ebony led them through the maze of ships until they reached a quiet corner. The back door of one ship lay open and they crept inside. Ferdy positioned himself behind the controls.

'Uh, Ferdy,' Dan said. 'Are you sure you should be doing that?'

'Doing what, Dan?' Ferdy asked.

'Shouldn't we just set the Flex to automatic?'

'That plan will not work,' Ferdy said. He manipulated a few controls before levering part of the console free. 'First of all, the automatic controls have been disengaged so that the craft cannot be stolen.'

'Oookaaay,' Ebony said.

'That is a standard Agency procedure.'

'Right.'

'Secondly, Ferdy must disengage the transponder so we cannot be tracked,' Ferdy continued. 'This vehicle seems to have suffered from an issue with its navigation system, although its other systems are fully operational.'

'Hmm.'

'Thirdly...'

'Yes, Ferdy.'

'The eighteenth element on the periodic table is argon.'

'Er...'

'That is a joke,' Ferdy said. 'Ferdy made a joke.'

'Ha ha ha.' Ebony's stomach was feeling queasy. 'Look, I really have to ask you—'

'Ferdy's friends must sit down,' Ferdy said. 'Security guards are approaching.'

'Oh, great,' Ebony said.

They sat. Within seconds Ferdy had started the engines of the Flex Fighter. It lifted up and swayed unnervingly from side to side. Ebony gripped her seat in panic as Ferdy accelerated the craft. They veered into a tunnel and Ebony caught a glimpse of a wall whizzing past. She caught a glimpse of Dan's face. He had gone pale and was desperately trying to fasten his seat belt.

'Ferdy,' Ebony said. 'Have you ever flown a Flex before?'

'Ferdy has flown a Flex Fighter many times.'

'Really?'

'There is a flight simulator in Ferdy's room,' he said. 'Ferdy used to crash it sometimes, but now he is a good pilot. He hardly ever crashes.'

'Hardly ever...'

Peering through the front window, Ebony could see the faraway entrance to the tunnel. She could see a patch of darkened sky and part of the desert. She frowned. The exit seemed to be contracting.

'The Agency is trying to stop our departure,' Ferdy said. 'They are closing the exit doors.'

'Well, what—'

The Flex Fighter shuddered and Ebony saw the trails of two missiles roar away from them. The projectiles slammed into the doors, blowing them apart. An instant later they flew through the exit and over the darkening desert. Open mouthed, Ebony peered back at the scattered remains of the doors.

'Ferdy is having fun,' Ferdy said. 'It is much more fun than throwing the ball.'

'I'm sure it is,' Ebony replied.

'Are Ebony and Dan having fun?'

'Uh, Dan's fainted.'

'Possibly Dan has had too much fun.'

'Maybe.'

'We must discard our cell phones,' Ferdy said. 'The Agency can track us through their transponder signals.'

Ebony nodded. Ferdy was right. She shook Dan into wakefulness, retrieved each of their phones and dropped them through a rear chute in the craft. Ferdy pushed a few more buttons on the display.

'Automatic pilot has not been re-engaged,' the computer said.

Ferdy smiled. 'Now we can find Brodie and Axel and Chad.'

Ebony turned to Dan. 'Now it's up to you. You were picking up something from Brodie earlier. Maybe you should try her again.'

Dan nodded. He closed his eyes and concentrated. After a minute he opened his eyes again. 'I'm not sure, but...I think I'm getting something.'

'What sort of something?' Ebony asked.

'An impression,' Dan said. 'I really do feel like a needle on a compass. I'm getting a sensation as to Brodie's direction.'

'Which way should we go?'

'You're going to find this a little hard to believe, but—'

'But what?'

'Up,' Dan said. 'We need to go up.'

The three of them peered through the front window.

'Brodie's either on an airplane,' Dan said. 'Or…'

'Or?'

'Or she's on a spaceship.'

Chapter Fourteen

'A spaceship?' Ebony asked.

'It is possible,' Ferdy said.

'That she's on a spaceship?'

Ferdy seemed lost in thought.

'Ferdy?' Ebony said.

'The distance from London to Melbourne is more than—'

'Try to stay focused, Ferdy.' She turned to Dan. 'Are you sure she's above us?'

Dan frowned. 'Yes. I'm sure.'

'Then Ferdy and his friends will have to go into space,' Ferdy said.

'Uh, how're we doing that?' Ebony asked.

'In this Flex.'

'Can one of these things go into space?' Dan asked.

'With the proper modifications.' Ferdy started to punch some buttons on the control panel. 'Ferdy will make the necessary adjustments.'

Ebony felt a queasy feeling in her stomach. This plan sounded suspiciously like they were courting disaster. It was one thing to go on a rescue mission to save Axel and the others; it was quite another matter to consider leaving the safety of Earth to go—where?

'I don't know about this,' she said uncertainly. 'I want to find the others, but this sounds like a suicide mission.'

'Friend Ebony,' Ferdy said. 'You need not be concerned about the ship's modifications. Ferdy has read the schematics of the changes and understands them completely.'

'But if something goes wrong—'

'Ferdy has calculated the problems that could arise,' Ferdy said. 'The most likely error would be an explosion that would kill us instantly—'

'Oh great.'

'—although we could survive in the vacuum of space for possibly another ninety seconds—'

'Wonderful.'

'—but our friends would do the same for us.' He stared into her eyes. 'Ralph Waldo Emerson said that, 'a friend may well be reckoned the masterpiece of nature.' Do Ebony and Dan not agree with this sentiment?'

Dan said nothing. He seemed stunned by the rapid turn of events. Ebony could not think of another plan. She leant back in the seat. 'Lead the way.'

Ferdy nodded. The Flex Fighter rose higher into the atmosphere. Ebony watched as the sky above turned darker until it was indigo and then finally black. The earth spread below them like a blanket. She found herself staring at the awe-inspiring spectacle in astonishment.

'It's so beautiful,' Ebony said.

'I'm getting an impression.' Dan rubbed his head. 'She is somewhere ahead of us.'

'Can Dan be more specific?' Ferdy asked. 'Most of the Milky Way galaxy is ahead of us.'

Dan shook his head. 'All is know is we're heading in the right direction.'

Ferdy manipulated the controls on the console. After a moment, Ebony felt the Flex gently accelerate.

'Ferdy has found it,' Ferdy said.

'What has Ferdy—' Ebony stopped. 'I mean, what have you found?'

'A spaceship,' he replied. 'It is some two miles in length. Ferdy believes that Brodie is aboard the ship.'

Peering through the window, Ebony saw a sharp speck of light above the blue horizon ahead of them. It grew larger with every second. The shape of it reminded her of the body of a cockroach; a smaller section dominated one end. Behind it lay two segmented compartments.

'It sure isn't the International Space Station,' Ebony said.

'Can't anyone see that thing from the Earth?' Dan asked.

'The ship is using stealth technology to hide it from ground radar,' Ferdy said. 'It is quite advanced, although not as advanced as the alien technology contained within The Agency's computer systems.'

'Uh,' Ebony said. 'Surely that's top secret.'

'It is.' He smiled. 'Ferdy circumvents the security protocols to access the information.'

'You hack The Agency computers?'

'Hacking is another definition for the same process,' Ferdy said. 'A zectometer is one of the smallest units of measurement.'

'You're not changing the subject, are you, Ferdy?'

'Ferdy would not do that.' Ferdy smiled. 'The largest mammal on Earth—'

The Flex Fighter shuddered as a high-pitched whine emanated from the engines.

'What's happening?' Dan asked.

'We are caught in a tractor beam,' Ferdy said. 'The alien spaceship is drawing us towards it.'

'They can see us?'

'The alien vessel is cloaked. Our vessel is visible to their systems.'

'Did you know this?' Ebony asked.

'Ferdy knew,' he confirmed. 'Should Ferdy have acted on that information?'

'Should Ferdy have—' Ebony fell back speechless in her seat. 'It might have been a good idea.'

'We will meet aliens,' Ferdy said. 'Possibly we will have fun.'

'Possibly,' Ebony said. 'But it's not likely.'

Chapter Fifteen

The desert had turned cold by the time I arrived at the rendezvous point to meet Graal. The sky above was inky black broken only by tiny pinpoints of light. It reminded me of a similar evening when Brodie and I had flown out to the desert to enjoy the stars.

A lump gathered in my throat. What if I never saw Brodie again? What if she was already dead? I had the Stonekiller secured in its case in a small pack strapped securely to my back. I would not hand it over until Brodie was safely—

A light split the air behind me. I had been facing a hill, but now I turned around to see the rear of a spaceship opening a few feet above the ground. Obviously the Tagaar vessel had been here the whole time. Cloaked.

Two figures strode down the ramp towards me. The first was Graal. I did not recognize the alien beside him.

'You are here,' Graal said. 'Good. I had my doubts whether you would escape The Agency in one piece.'

'Where's Brodie?'

'All in good time.'

'No! I will give you the weapon, but only if you release her!'

Graal shook his head. 'You misunderstand me, my young friend. I do not want the weapon.'

'Then why—'

'You will need the Stonekiller for your next assignment,' Graal said. 'We will release your mate once your assignment is completed.'

'But you promised—'

'I gave no such promise.' The alien produced an object from his pouch. 'However, as a sign of good faith, I will allow you to speak to the girl.'

He pointed the object into the air. A square panel formed before us. I could see the interior of a cell. People were lying on the floor. They looked up.

'Brodie!' I said.

I stepped forward and my hand intersected with the image. It passed straight through. This was some sort of holographic projection. Brodie leapt to her feet.

'Axel?' she said. 'What is this? How are—'

'Are you all right?' I asked.

'I'm on a spaceship,' she said. 'I'm in a cell onboard—'

The image faded and I found myself staring at Graal's face. He looked pleased with himself. I wanted to kill him. I had never felt such rage in my life, yet I was able to force it down deep into my stomach.

'Good,' Graal said. 'I see your hatred. A warrior needs such emotions or he will not survive.'

'Shut up!' A red haze of fury blurred my vision. 'What must I do?'

'You have no doubt heard of Alexi Kozlov?'

I searched my memory. 'The Russian Premier?'

'He is to be your target.'

'The leader of Russia?' I felt light-headed. 'That's insane.'

'You will shoot him with the Stonekiller and return with him to this place. You will do these things or your mate will die.'

I took an enraged step towards him.

'Do not be foolish, boy,' Graal said. 'Your mate will be returned if you follow my instructions. You have my promise. I will also promise to throw her out of an airlock into space if you refuse my instructions.'

'How would I ever get close enough—'

'I have already uploaded a map to your compass,' the alien said. 'He was tagged with a non-invasive tracking device several days ago. You will track him using the device.'

'But it's the Russian Premier!' I blurted. 'How will I—'

'You will do what is required,' Graal said.

I stood in the cold desert for several seconds, consumed by desperation and hatred and fear. My hands were clenched so tightly I could feel my fingernails cutting into the palms of my hands. Finally I crossed a barrier. A point of no-return. I would not let Brodie down. I could not let her die.

'And if I do this?

'Your mate will be returned.'

'Why don't you kill him yourself?' I asked. 'If you were able to place a tracker—'

'That is not our way,' Graal said. 'A countdown has been activated on your compass. You have two of your Earth days. We will meet here again when the countdown reaches zero.' He paused. 'And we will bring your mate.'

'Her name is Brodie,' I said.

Graal responded by ignoring me and turning away. He disappeared up into the ship. The ramp slid away into nothingness and a moment later I heard the engines of the spaceship burst into life. Wind rushed against my face as the invisible vessel lifted off the ground. I saw a faint shimmer distort the sea of stars as it raced across the sky.

I stood in the silent desert, cold and alone. I could get Brodie back, but I would have to sentence a man to a fate worse than death to do it.

Chapter Sixteen

It was the longest journey of my life.

I left in darkness and I arrived in darkness. Judging by the device on my wrist, it appeared that Alexi Kozlov was located somewhere to the south of Moscow. As I neared my destination, the darkened landscape slowly morphed into hills, towns, roads and rivers. I descended slowly, eventually landing in a forested area outside a small village. A farmhouse with a dilapidated barn lay nearby; I could just make out a faint light in one of the windows.

A dog barked distantly. The faraway engine of a truck growled into life. A bird took flight in a nearby tree and disappeared to parts unknown.

I felt exhausted. I had flown for fifteen hours straight. My head ached. My back ached. A cramp painfully cinched my left thigh. Checking my watch, I realized it was about nine in the evening. I sat back against a tree. I needed rest. I would sleep for a minute, but no longer.

Just a minute…

When I awoke, most of the night had passed.

Panicked, I examined the timer on the compass. Nine hours had passed. I tried to calm my breathing. I still had enough time to complete my mission.

My mission...

A deep well of misery opened up within me. I had betrayed my friends. I had destroyed my relationship with The Agency. I could never go back to the life I had led. To get Brodie back I would have to consign a stranger to a fate worse than death. *And that stranger was the Premier of Russia!* What would be the repercussions of carrying out such an attack?

My actions could start a war.

My stomach rolled over at the thought. I absently wiped tears from my face as I made out a faint glow on the distant horizon. Dawn. Soon it would be day and then I would deal with the next phase of this nightmare. I had to wait for daylight to arrive. It was bad enough bumbling about in a foreign country. Trying to consider assassinating—and it was a type of assassination—someone in the middle of the night was ridiculous.

'So,' a voice said from behind me. 'Sleeping

Beauty is finally awake.'

I scrambled to my feet and readied myself for an attack. At the same time, however, my weary brain recognized the voice.

A figure moved from behind a tree.

Chad.

'A bit of advice,' he said. 'When you're on the run, look behind you sometimes. You'll live longer that way.'

'Thanks. I'll keep that in mind.' I peered into the darkened forest behind him. 'How did you keep up with me?'

'You remember that Flex that disappeared from The Agency a few months back?'

'Yeah.'

'That was me,' he said. 'And Ferdy.'

'You and Ferdy stole a Flex Fighter?'

'I hid it in the desert,' he said. 'Just in case.'

'Looks like it came in handy.'

He ignored me. 'I heard the conversation you had with your alien buddies.'

'They're not my friends.'

'I know.' Chad paused. 'I've been following you for hours.'

'So you know they've got Brodie.'

He nodded. 'And you're supposed to take out the Russian leader with—'

'The Stonekiller weapon.' The words sounded foreign to my lips. 'It doesn't actually kill the person. It freezes them so they can't move.'

'Sounds great.' He shook his head. 'You can't mean to—'

'I don't have a choice! They'll kill Brodie if I don't do as they say!'

'But it's the Premier of Russia,' Chad said. 'You could start a war!'

'I know.' I felt miserable. 'But I can't let Brodie die!'

'Look, Axel,' he said. 'I'm not suggesting you should. But you can't just consign someone to a living death.'

I turned away. In my heart, I knew what he was saying was right. I looked up at the horizon. The sky was growing brighter by the moment. Three shapes moved across a distant row of roofs.

'You have to trust your friends,' Chad said. 'We're stronger as a team—'

'I just saw something,' I said. 'I think someone's—watch out!'

A bright plume of fire arced across the sky towards us. I threw a shield up as it slammed into the ground. The earth beneath us exploded, throwing us backward. Trees and dirt flew in all directions.

I struggled to my feet. I could see two figures in the gloomy field beyond the tree line.

'American spies!' one of them called out. 'You will surrender yourselves for interrogation.'

I didn't like the sound of any of that. I never like it when the words spies, surrender and interrogation are used at the same time.

'We're not spies!' Chad yelled. 'We're lost. And I'm not American.'

'I don't think that will make any difference to them,' I said.

It was growing lighter by the minute. Now the two figures were clearer. They were men. One wore red. The other wore blue. Something jangled at the back of my mind. The Russian flag was three horizontal stripes. Red, blue and—

The world turned upside down.

One second I was turning around to look behind us. The next I found the world spinning sideways and I could not tell up from down. I felt like I was falling, yet my feet were still planted firmly on the ground.

What the hell was going on?

'Vertigo,' I heard Chad's voice come from somewhere behind me—or was he in front of me? 'This guy has the powers of disorientation.'

I understood. Through a gap in the trees I saw a man in a white uniform. His hand was outstretched. Obviously he had some sort of power that disrupted the inner ear. I raised my hand to throw a cannonball of air at him, but the world flipped over again.

Chad hurled a blast of fire and I heard a scream. Crashing face first into the ground, I felt a sharp pain in my nose. It might have been broken. At least now I knew up from down. As we climbed to our feet, we saw the man rolling about on the ground. He looked singed, but otherwise uninjured.

We turned. Red and Blue were charging towards us. Throwing out an arm, Blue hurled a bolt of electricity at us. I threw myself to one side, but heard a cry as Chad was hit. He fell to the ground.

'Chad!' I screamed.

He didn't move as the three men closed in around me.

I would have to deal with them.

Alone.

Chapter Seventeen

'Faster!' the alien growled.

The alien hit Ferdy in the back of the head with the butt of his gun.

Ebony protested. 'Hey! Leave him alone. He doesn't understand.'

She took Ferdy's hand and moved him away from the alien. Dan was behind them. Shepherded by the guards, they moved through the dimly lit corridors of the spaceship. Events had occurred rather rapidly since their Flex Fighter had been dragged into the alien ship's landing bay. Dan had wanted to fight their way out of the vessel, but Ebony could immediately see a dozen holes in the plan.

Ferdy had super strength, but he was almost impossible to co-ordinate in a fight. She and Dan had powers, but they could not take on an alien ship with hundreds—or thousands—of soldiers on board. Besides, they were here to find Brodie. It seemed to make more sense to wait and see what would happen.

Unfortunately, not much had happened since then. They had been shoved into a cell before another alien had turned up to move them again. He had introduced himself as T'bar.

'I am second in command,' he said. 'I know you have powers, but I would advise you to cooperate. It is impossible to escape this ship.'

'Where are we being taken?' Ebony asked.

'You are to fight,' T'bar said.

'Who are we fighting?'

'Our Tagaar warriors.'

Ebony didn't like the sound of that. 'What have you done with our friend?'

'The girl?' the alien said. 'She has proven quite an adversary.'

Good, Ebony thought. *So Brodie's still alive.*

'We're an adversarial race,' she said.

'You will be overcome by the Tagaar,' T'bar said. 'As are all races we encounter.'

Just what we needed, Ebony thought. *Invaders from Mars!*

They reached a closed door. The alien unlocked it and motioned them inside. Ebony was about to protest when she peered into the chamber.

'Brodie!' she screamed.

They rushed into the cell. Brodie threw her arms around them as the alien watched impassively from the doorway.

'I will return shortly,' T'bar said. 'One of you will be chosen to fight.'

'Ferdy will fight you,' Ferdy said. 'Ferdy is not afraid.'

T'bar leveled his gaze at him. 'You will be, boy.'

'The first flight of the Wright Brothers was one hundred and twenty feet,' Ferdy told him.

'The fear has addled your mind,' the alien said and slammed the door shut.

'I'm so glad to see you guys,' Brodie said. 'But how did you get here?'

They all spoke at once. Brodie held up her hands.

'One at a time,' she said. 'Please.'

Ebony explained the rapid sequence of events that had led them to the alien craft. Brodie listened in silence until she finally nodded.

'That explains a few things,' she said. 'Some sort of communications window opened up in here briefly. I could see and speak to Axel.'

'The Agency is treating him like a criminal,' Dan said.

'The Tagaar are blackmailing him,' Brodie said.

'Who are the Tagaar?'

Brodie explained what she knew of the alien race.

'What happened to your face?' Dan asked.

Brodie gingerly touched her bruised cheek. 'The Tagaar love nothing more than to fight. I've fought three times so far.'

'And she has succeeded,' a voice came from the rear of the darkened cell. 'She is more of a warrior than any of them.'

They turned to see two aliens step from the shadows.

'This is Zena and Bax,' Brodie introduced them. 'They have been my companions here.'

'Your friend is strong,' Zena said. 'You will

need to be strong to defeat the Tagaar.'

They sat around in a circle in the middle of the cell as Zena related her tale of what had happened to her world. The more Ebony looked at Brodie, the more she realized how battered her friend looked. Finally she asked Brodie about the fights.

'The Tagaar are tough,' Brodie said. 'And they know how to fight.'

'We'll beat them,' Dan said.

'That is unlikely, friend Dan,' Ferdy said. 'The Tagaar appear to have technology far more advanced than any developed on Earth.'

'We can't give up, Ferdy,' Ebony said.

'We will not give up,' he said. 'But the way ahead will be difficult and our goals will not be achieved without sacrifices.'

'You sound like you can see the future,' Dan said.

'Ferdy is very smart,' he said. 'Ferdy can extrapolate many possible versions of the future. We must wait and see in what direction our path lies.'

'The first thing we need to do is get back to

Earth,' Brodie said.

'There's about a million Tagaar warriors between us and our ship,' Dan said.

'Plus they've got their tractor beam,' Ebony added.

Brodie turned to Ferdy. 'Can you work out a way to deflect their tractor beam?'

'Ferdy has been thinking about this,' he replied. 'Ferdy has also been thinking about the role of superstring theory when contemplating the—'

'Ferdy,' Ebony interrupted.

He nodded. 'A modulating pulse can be transmitted through the hull that will deflect the Tagaar tractor beam. It has an eighty percent chance of success.'

'What about the other twenty percent?' Dan asked.

'There is a seventeen percent chance the pulse will fail and the ship will not escape,' Ferdy explained. 'And a three percent chance the ship will explode, killing everyone on board.'

'Always with the good news...' Brodie

murmured.

'I've got a plan,' Dan said.

'What is it?' Brodie asked.

'It always works in the movies,' Dan said excitedly. 'We'll pretend you're sick and you need a doctor. When the guards come in we'll overpower them and steal their guns.'

Ferdy crossed to the door. 'Or we can just knock the door down.'

He hit the door and it exploded outward into the hall. The unfortunate guards who were standing on the other side of it were slammed to the ground and did not move. Everyone inside the cell peered into the hallway in amazement.

'Your friend is very strong,' Zena said.

'As well as intelligent,' Bax added.

'He doesn't know his own talents,' Ebony explained. 'Come on.'

As they all poured into the hallway, Brodie and Zena snatched up the weapons of the fallen warriors.

'Which way?' Ebony asked.

'The shuttle bay is in this direction.' Ferdy pointed.

They hurried down the corridor. Brodie wondered about their chances of escaping from the ship. Or even surviving this situation. So much had happened so quickly. Then there was the issue with Axel. If he had stolen a weapon from The Agency she doubted he would ever be welcomed back.

They turned a corner—and encountered a squad of Tagaar warriors heading in their direction.

'Damn,' Brodie said. 'It's showtime.'

Chapter Eighteen

Morgan Le Fay sat at the bow of the small cruiser as it bounced across the waves of the North Sea towards Cargall Island. Once or twice the two men in charge of the ship had left the safety of the wheel house to invite her back to the warm interior.

'Not right now.' She smiled. 'I love the sea.'

They would then nod uncertainly and hurry back inside. Morgan could understand their confusion. It was freezing on the water and she was dressed in little more than a summer dress. Anyone else would have collapsed from frostbite.

Of course, she was not anyone else.

Morgan Le Fay let out a sigh. She was tired of her exile on this backwater planet. She needed to be free, and her alliance with the Tagaar would achieve that goal.

The Tagaar are stupid, she thought. *But they are powerful.*

If there was one thing Morgan had learnt over the centuries, it was that stupid people often gained power with surprising ease. She had met Oliver

Cromwell once and he had said something that had stayed with her ever since.

'Power belongs to those who are prepared to take it,' he said.

The Tagaar were stupid, but they saw the Earth as an opportunity and they were prepared to take it. She needed them. So be it. She had known the Tagaar would come to Earth sooner or later. Now that time had arrived, and deep down inside she felt an emotion that was as foreign to her as the day of her birth.

Fear.

She knew when to abandon ship, and that time was now. The Earth was finished. Certainly she would still enjoy a few more years of murdering and torturing innocent people, but then the Tagaar would increase their stranglehold on the planet. Sooner or later the human race would be reduced to slaves, and for Morgan Le Fay, it was a fate to which she would not yield.

The south coast of Cargall Island was growing larger by the moment. They would reach it within the hour. She strode back along the deck to the wheelhouse where the two men were huddled inside. They looked at her in amazement as she stepped inside from the freezing cold.

'Are ye not frozen, madam?' the captain asked.

She gave both men a smile. What were their names again? She had gotten terribly forgetful of late. There had been so many people over the centuries; after a while they all blended together into one feast with so many different courses.

Ah yes.

Seamus the captain and his brother Donald.

AKA dinner and dessert!

'It is cold,' Morgan agreed. 'Do you go to the island often?'

'Only to drop off supplies,' Donald said. He was slouched up against the opposite wall, his thumbs hitched into his faded blue jeans. His eyes were firmly fixed on Morgan's body. He continued. 'The scientists are always getting new pieces of equipment for their contraption out there.'

'The Solar Accelerator,' Morgan said. 'A very interesting device.'

'If you say so,' Donald said.

Captain Seamus shot a warning look at his brother before focusing on Morgan. 'And what takes you to Cargall Island?'

'I have an interest in particle physics,' Morgan said.

'Really?' The captain looked as if such a thing were ridiculous. 'It's hard to believe that a…well…a…'

'A beautiful woman would be interested in such things?' Morgan asked.

Seamus felt distinctly uncomfortable and kept his focus resolutely ahead. They were almost at the island now. Like his brother, he found the woman attractive. Unlike his brother, he also thought her dangerous. Who in their right mind would remain at the bow of the ship in sub-zero temperatures? It was insane. Yet the woman seemed perfectly contented with standing in their wheel room in a dripping wet dress. It was nothing short of…bizarre.

They finally reached the small jetty that jutted out into the cove on the east side of the island. Donald went up to the bow and tied the small boat to one of the mooring stumps. Morgan turned to the captain.

'Will you be so kind as to come up to the dock?' she asked.

The captain looked puzzled but nodded. They had not been paid yet. He followed her up onto the jetty. The weather had worsened and the rain was now falling harder than ever. Morgan seemed not to notice it at all. The men looked at her expectantly.

'There's the matter of payment,' Seamus said.

'Of course,' Morgan replied. 'At first I thought I would consume both of you, but I've since decided you are both too disgusting.'

Seamus stared at her dumbly. He had been right. The woman was mad. He opened his mouth to reply, but found he could not make a sound. Nor could he move a muscle. He looked across at Donald and realized his brother was in a similar predicament. A low cry of terror emanated from deep within his throat, but was quickly swept away by the wind.

'You men are very dirty,' Morgan said. 'A dip will do you both the world of good.'

Both men walked stiff-legged to the edge of the jetty.

'Swim to the bottom,' Morgan told them. 'And don't come back.'

The men dove into the water. They disappeared from view within seconds, but Morgan remained on the edge of the jetty for several minutes, imagining the terror of the men as they clung to the rocky bottom of the cove until they drowned.

Only then did she start up the path leading to the town.

Chapter Nineteen

The three Russian superheroes advanced on me. I didn't want to fight them. I didn't want to hurt anyone. I only wanted to get on with my mission.

But none of that was possible.

The one in the blue outfit said something in Russian to me. I did my best to look dazed—which was easy under the circumstances—and closed my eyes. Taking a deep breath, I focused. A breath of air moved against my cheek.

The wind built slowly. At first it was simply a breeze in the trees; the branches shuffled slightly in the early morning air. Then it built up rapidly. I opened my eyes to see Red looking up at the trees in confusion.

Now, I thought. *Now!*

The hurricane hit with full ferocity. I kept myself and Chad at the heart of the storm as it swept around us. Red fired another bolt of electricity, but it went wild. Blue gave a single wave of his arms before he was lifted off his feet. He flew past us like something out of the Wizard of Oz. Trees were ripped out by the roots.

Chad slowly lifted his head. 'What hit me?'

'Some guy in a red suit.'

'Who? Santa Claus?'

'I don't think so. Anyway, he and his friends are out of the picture.'

Chad climbed to his feet as I brought the wind under control. It subsided to nothing. All around us lay the devastated forest, but there was no sign of the Russians. I doubted the storm had killed them, but it had probably left them incapacitated.

We hurried past the farmhouse and followed a road down into a small village. An old man stuck his head out from the upper window of a building and disappeared again just as quickly.

'We need to lay low,' I said.

'You need to lay low. I'm just a tourist here.'

'Fine.'

'No need to be snappy.'

'I'm not.'

'I was just wondering how you intend to get close to the Premier.'

It was a good question. Studying the compass, it appeared the Russian Premier was about two kilometers south of our position. He was probably visiting the area on a re-election tour. I remembered seeing references to the upcoming ballot on television. I could not fly. The Russian Defense Force was probably watching the skies. This was looking worse by the moment. My eyes settled on a manhole cover in the ground.

'That's how we'll do it,' I said.

'How's that?'

I hurried across to the manhole cover and lifted it with a gust of air. A ladder led down into darkness, but I could vaguely make out a tunnel leading in the right direction. I turned to Chad.

'Do you have a torch?'

He produced a flame at the end of his finger.

'Okay,' I said. 'Stupid question.'

We descended the ladder, dragging the cover back over behind us. This was a storm drain. Fortunately it had not rained for a while; only a thin line of water ran down the center of the circular channel. I checked the map again as we started down the tunnel. Silence closed in around us. The world above was only a few feet away, yet it might as well have been miles away. The quiet was unnerving. The only sound was that of our steps in the passageway. Occasionally our feet would splash in the thin trail of water and it sounded like the breaking of glass.

We did not speak. I wondered what was going through Chad's mind. A few days ago our lives had seemed set in stone. We were working at the behest of The Agency. We had a place to live and food to eat. Now I had thrown all that away. At least Chad still had his life. He could turn around and go back home. To stay with me was pure insanity.

'It looks like this tunnel will take us right into the center of the town,' I said. 'You should leave once we reach the surface.'

'How do you work that out?' Chad's voice reverberated around the interior of the tunnel. 'Do you think you can take on the entire Russian army yourself?'

'This isn't your fight,' I said.

'Brodie's in trouble,' he replied. 'That makes it my fight.'

'But when I use the weapon—'

'I know.' He sounded angry. 'It's a fate worse than death. I get that. I don't agree with how you've handled this whole—'

'I know I—'

'You should have trusted us,' he interrupted. 'We could have worked together to save her.'

'Her life is at stake,' I said. 'I'm in love with her.'

That shut him up for a moment. Then he said, 'You don't show it.'

'What do you mean?'

'Half the time, you ignore her,' he said. 'The other half of the time you spend with Ebony.'

'What?'

'You heard me,' he said. 'You spend more time with Ebony than with Brodie.'

I was about to protest, but there was some truth in what he was saying. If I was in love with Brodie, I had a funny way of showing it. It wasn't that I had those sorts of feelings for Ebony. She was a friend. That was all. She had certainly not shown any romantic interest in me. So was I really in love with Brodie or was I—

A sound came from the tunnel behind us. I threw up a shield—and not a moment too soon. A shape raced towards us. It was Blue. He hit my shield and the barrier held—but only just. He started pounding the shield so hard I thought he was about to break through it. Even Chad looked scared.

'Keep moving!' I yelled.

We backed up the tunnel away from him. Chad threw up a wall of ice several feet thick and we made a run for it. As we reached a bend in the passageway, I glanced back to see the icy wall being demolished.

He came charging at us again.

We sprinted down the tunnel with Blue in pursuit. I heard him accelerating on us. This tunnel was turning out to be a bad idea. It was too confining. To make matters worse, I didn't want to harm Blue or the other superheroes. They were just doing their job.

I heard an explosion from behind me.

'That should stop him,' Chad said.

I turned to see a wall of fire behind us. Chad had formed it to stop Blue from pursuing us. At least it would—

Blue crashed straight through it as if it weren't there and slammed into Chad. Hard. I heard Chad give a grunt of pain as he hit the ground. I threw a cannonball of air at Blue, but it didn't slow him down. What was this guy? Indestructible? The man continued towards me and I threw up another invisible barrier. This slowed him down, but not much. He continued straining to reach me. Pounding the invisible barrier, he reminded me of some sort of enraged gorilla.

Chad somehow got to his feet and threw more ice at Blue, but this time he embedded the Russian inside. The problem now was that there was no room for Chad to join me; the solid block of man and ice was between me and him.

'Keep going!' Chad yelled.

'I can't leave you behind!' I said.

'You've got to,' he said. 'For Brodie.'

There was no time to argue. Chad was right. The longer I stayed here, the lesser the chance I would achieve my mission. I ran down the corridor. Within minutes I located a ladder to the surface. Just before I started to climb, I heard the sound of crashing ice.

Chad was on his own.

Chapter Twenty

We're not going to make it, Brodie thought.

They had headed in the direction of the landing bay and already encountered two groups of Tagaar warriors. Since gaining her superpowers, Brodie had faced some difficult opponents, but none were as formidable as the Tagaar. She had been forced to beat a number of them into unconsciousness during her one-on-one fights. Now she and the others faced the same sort of opposition as they now struggled to get to the landing bay.

Must be their thick skulls, she thought. *They don't know when to stop.*

They rounded the corner and came face to face with another group of warriors. Ferdy had ripped an enormous piece of metal from the hull and now used it as a shield. They took refuge behind it as the Tagaar group fired and advanced. Finally they came face to face with the warriors and the aliens breached the shield and engaged in hand to hand combat. As Brodie fought one of the warriors, she saw all her friends—except Ferdy—engaged in similar battles.

Ferdy simply stood by and watched the mayhem taking place around him.

Dan and Ebony used their combined powers to bring down one warrior. Zena and Bax took on a warrior each. Within seconds the Tagaar were defeated. Brodie and the others continued down the corridor, turned a corner—and were faced with another group of warriors.

'Are they making these things out of Lego?' Dan asked. 'There are so many of them.'

'How far are we from the shuttle bay?' Ebony asked.

'Approximately half a kilometre,' Ferdy said. 'If I were to calculate that in inches, it would be—'

'Later!' Brodie yelled.

A shot came from behind them.

'Gark!' Bax swore.

Another group of warriors were coming up the tunnel behind them. Brodie and the others opened fire, but one of the warriors let loose a volley at the same time and Ebony cried out. She hit the ground, gripping her shoulder. Dan quickly focused on the roof and tore loose a section. He propelled it towards the warriors and it slammed into them, knocking them over like bowling pins.

'I'm okay,' Ebony said through gritted teeth.

Brodie examined the wound. 'The hell you are.'

'We've got to keep moving,' Zena said.

'We're not going to make it to the shuttle bay,' Dan said. 'There's too many of them.'

Brodie examined Ebony's wound. She had a bad burn across her right shoulder.

'We've got to go sideways,' Dan said. 'Like in Star Wars.'

'Huh?' Brodie said. 'Which one?'

'The first one,' Dan said. 'It's when they rescue Princess Leia and they are trying to escape from the storm troopers.'

He pointed at a piece of paneling on the wall and tore it loose. A shaft, descending into darkness, lay beyond. Brodie didn't feel comfortable about jumping into the unknown, but the Tagaar troops were growing closer with every second.

'All right.' She made a snap decision. 'Let's do it.'

Bax and Zena went first. They were followed by Dan and Ebony. Brodie grabbed Ferdy's arm and pointed down the tube.

'Okay, Ferdy,' she said. 'It's your turn.'

He looked down the shaft. 'It is very dark.'

'Now is not the time to be a scaredy cat.'

'I am not any sort of feline. Cats are descended from—'

'Take my hand.' Brodie dragged him to the gap. 'We're going at the count of three. One, two—'

She jumped, dragging Ferdy down the tube behind her. The shaft closed in around them. It fell straight down for several meters before they hit a bump and it angled out into a steep incline. A stench hit her. It smelt like garbage.

It's just like Star Wars, she thought. *We're going to land in a garbage dump. Wait a second. Wasn't there a monster in—*

A red glare appeared ahead of them and in the next instant they fell through a gap. For an instant they were in mid-air. Then they rebounded off some kind of roof and fell through a hole into what appeared to be the living room of some sort of shanty hut. Brodie looked up to see everyone standing around, rubbing their bumps and bruises. Ebony helped her to her feet.

'Ferdy was in the air,' Ferdy said. 'Ferdy was flying.'

'You were indeed,' Brodie said. 'Now, where are we?'

'You are in Sartaria,' a voice said from behind them.

The man in the doorway was humanoid in shape, but he was covered in a fine light brown fur. He had a snub nose and eyes set widely apart.

'I have heard of this place,' Zena said. 'It is the slave section of this Tagaar ship.'

He nodded.

'There are people from a hundred different worlds in this place,' he said. 'My name is Tomay. I am a member of the Council.'

'You said this is the slave section,' Ebony

said. 'What do you do down here?'

'We work in the foundries for the Tagaar,' Tomay said. 'We build parts for cannons and other equipment.'

For the first time, Brodie noticed the heat. It was stifling, and the smell in the air—

Her thoughts about the garbage dump were not so far from being true. She peered upward, realizing they had smashed through the roof of a makeshift home. The darkened shaft lay behind them. Returning through it would prove impossible; it was too steep to climb.

'We need to get out of here,' Brodie said. 'Can you help us?'

Tomay shook his head sadly. 'There is no escaping from Sartaria.'

'The guards must come down here sometimes,' Dan said. 'Surely we can overpower them—'

'They have weapons,' Tomay said. 'They will simply kill anyone who stands against them. Sometimes they kill someone at random to simply set an example.'

That's terrible, Brodie thought. *The Tagaar are monsters!*

A chill ran down her spine. Now they intended to do the same thing to Earth! What role did the Bakari play in all this? Wasn't there supposed to be a Union of Planets? What was the Union doing?

She asked Tomay about this and was surprised by his response.

'The Union is mostly ineffectual,' he said. 'They meet and set rules and make laws, but they lack the military might to enforce their rulings.'

'So they're like a toothless tiger,' Brodie said.

Tomay looked at her in confusion.

'It sounds tough,' Brodie explained. 'But it has no bite.'

The alien nodded. 'And now you're in Sartaria. The land of the slaves.'

They followed him out of the dwelling. They stood in a narrow alley with similar falling-down buildings lining both sides of it. The roof curved high above them; its highest reaches lay in complete darkness. They had been lucky to fall through an air shaft where the ceiling almost met the floor. Casting her eye across the chaotic landscape, Brodie saw various light sources illuminating the gloom. A shower of bright yellow sparks erupted from somewhere to their left.

That must be a furnace, Brodie thought. *One of the places where they build Tagaar equipment.*

The air was thick with smoke and strange odors. A family walked past them, giving them a curious look.

'They are Densai,' Bax said.

'Their world was completely destroyed by the Tagaar,' Tomay said.

'When you say completely destroyed…' Dan's voice trailed off.

'The Densai fought long and hard against the Tagaar,' Tomay explained. 'The Tagaar wished to make an example of the Densai to warn others who might stand against them. They ignited the atmosphere of their planet. It killed every living thing on the surface. To complete the process they drilled through to the core of the world and exploded it from within.'

'That's terrible,' Ebony said, feeling ill.

'I think we need to—' Tomay started.

A group of men came hurrying around a corner in the settlement and headed straight for them.

'That is Ragin,' Tomay said quietly. 'He is another member of the Council.'

'So it is true,' Ragin said as the group drew near. He was a tall, pale gray man with large eyes. 'There are strangers in Sartaria.'

'We didn't mean to intrude—' Brodie started.

Ragin cut her off. 'It is too late for that. You have already brought trouble.'

'What do you mean?' Ebony asked.

'The Tagaar soldiers are in the main square,' Ragin said. 'They are demanding that we hand you over.'

'And if you don't?' Dan asked.

'If we do not,' he said, 'they will execute one of us every hour.'

Chapter Twenty-One

I was standing in a small lane in the early morning light. I felt terrible about leaving Chad behind, but there was nothing else I could have done. Peering down at the wrist compass, I saw that the Russian Premier was nearby—and on the move. He and his security forces had probably been warned of my approach.

I flew straight up into the sky. I had been worried before about the authorities catching sight of me, but I was beyond that now. There was only one direction, and that was forward.

Hovering over the town, I looked for movement on the landscape and found it immediately. A convoy was leaving the other side of the village. It was comprised of a dozen jeeps and personnel carriers. In the midst of it was a limousine.

My stomach turned over uncomfortably. It wasn't so much at the thought of taking on the convoy—although that was difficult enough. It was what awaited me if I succeeded. I would have to use the Stonekiller weapon on the Premier of Russia and then—

And then my whole life would never be the same again.

Creating a shield around me, I started towards the convoy. A gunshot rang out; they had already seen me. I swung around behind the convoy as the firing continued. Soon an angry hail of bullets was rebounding off me. The convoy accelerated out of the town, followed a road through a field and into a thickly wooded area. I hung back and waited until it reached the forest. It would be more difficult for me to maneuver in the woods, but it would also be harder for them to spot me.

Waiting until the convoy reached the heart of the wood, I focused on one of the trees near the road. Building up an enormous gust of wind, I applied some force and it fell with an almighty crash behind the limousine. The vehicles behind it screeched to a halt. Stranded. Only a few armored cars remained in front of the luxury automobile.

A rocket flew out of nowhere at me. A launcher must have been on one of the lead vehicles. I flew erratically through the trees, but it still pursued me. Flying high above the field, I created a cannonball of air and propelled it straight towards the rocket.

Ka-boom!

The shockwave knocked me flying for a few seconds. I shook my head to clear it before once again sighting the remaining convoy. Good. The rear vehicles were still stranded behind the fallen tree. Now I only had to focus on the others.

I zoomed straight down again and blasted another tree, but this time the remaining vehicles were too fast. They whizzed past before it struck the road. A rocket raced towards me, but I blasted it out of the air before it drew too close. Making up for lost time, I sped after the convoy and knocked another tree to the ground. This one crashed into the bonnet of the limousine, dragging the car to a halt. The remaining vehicles slammed their brakes on, but I threw a hurricane blast at them. Within seconds the vehicles had rolled and crashed into the forest.

Agents leapt out of the front and back of the

limousine. They screamed something in Russian and started firing at me. My shield held. If it failed for even a second, I would be cut to pieces by the barrage of bullets. I knocked the men to one side as I advanced on the car.

I grabbed the handle of the middle door, but it did not move.

Damn.

They were going to make me fight them every step of the way.

Focusing on the tiny gaps of air between the door and the frame of the vehicle, I expanded the air until the door shuddered and broke loose. I grabbed it and threw it to one side. At the same time I was hit by another hail of bullets. This time it was from the two occupants of the vehicle. A man and a woman.

I had not expected a woman. I looked at her dumbly. Of course, she was the Premier's wife. Ivana. I saw an expression of utter terror on her face. My first thought was to console her, but then I realized that was simply ridiculous. I was here to consign her husband to a living death. There were no words that could candy coat that fact. Knocking the guns from their hands, I reached in and knocked out the Premier with a single punch. They had been teaching me how to make my blows more powerful by constructing an invisible glove around my hand. I never knew I would use my training against an innocent man.

The Premier sagged in the seat. Reaching for him, Ivana screamed something at me and started slapping at me with her bare fists. None of the blows struck me, but I was all too aware of her hysteria.

I threw the Premier over my shoulder and withdrew from the vehicle. A number of soldiers had gathered around the vehicle, but someone who looked like a captain barked out an order. They would not fire for fear of hitting the Premier. I zoomed straight up into the sky.

I had him. Now I had to find a place to use the Stonekiller on him. Fortunately the wood in which I had stopped the vehicle was large. After a few minutes of flying, I located a small clearing. I crashed into the soft earth untidily. The effects of the last few days were beginning to take their toll on me. As I lowered the Premier to the ground, I felt him stir and he swung about wildly. He landed a punch in the middle of my face.

Everything went white for a moment. He had taken me off-guard. Without my shield up, I was as vulnerable as anyone. Releasing him, I hit the ground hard. He turned to run, but I recovered quickly, knocking his feet out from under him with a blast of air. He landed face first into the soft ground. Wiping a line of blood from my nose, I struggled to remove the Stonekiller from my backpack.

Alexi Kozlov rolled over and looked up at me with a mixture of fear and hatred. 'You Americans are foolish to make this attack,' he said. 'Russia will retaliate with all of its might. You cannot kill me without expecting terrible repercussions.'

'I know there will be repercussions,' I said.

Pointing the gun at him, I began to squeeze the trigger.

Chapter Twenty-Two

'That's blackmail!' Dan said. 'And evil…and bad…and...'

Tomay looked at him sadly. 'The Tagaar are not concerned with morals. They only know of one thing, and that is domination.'

'You cannot hand us over,' Brodie said. 'We are innocent—'

'Everyone here is innocent. We have all lost friends and family and worlds to the Tagaar. I'm not sure how much more we can lose.' His bottom lip trembled. 'But the decision is not mine to make. We must hold an emergency meeting of the Council to discuss this matter.'

Ragin looked like discussion was the last thing on his mind. 'What are these people to us that we must make—'

'The Council must decide!' Tomay snapped. He turned to Brodie and the others. 'I will ask you to follow me to the Council Chambers.'

'I appreciate the offer,' Brodie said. 'But we should probably just leave.'

'Leave?' Ragin looked at her in amazement. 'Child, none of us would be here if we could simply leave!'

'There must be a way out,' Ebony said. 'There was certainly a way in.'

She pointed up at the hole in the ventilation shaft.

'The guards will repair that shortly,' Tomay said. 'And there is no way to return up the chute. And even if there were—what then? Where would we go?'

Brodie was getting a little tired of this negative attitude, but she reminded herself that these people had been through a lot. They had lost their worlds and they had been reduced to slavery. Besides, it was one thing to try to return to their Flex Fighter. It was quite another to plan a mass evacuation of thousands of people.

'Come to the Council Chambers,' he said. 'There you will be able to present your argument.'

Brodie nodded to the others. 'I think we should go.'

They followed in silence through a labyrinth

of shanty town structures. Brodie peered into the structures as they passed. Some people were cooking food. Others were sleeping. Everyone looked demoralized.

Brodie decided to try to break through Ragin's defensive attitude. 'It must be very hard for you down here.'

Ragin nodded without speaking.

'How many people live in Sartaria?' Brodie persisted.

'Too many,' Ragin said. 'Almost fifty thousand.'

'Fifty thousand?' Brodie was astounded. 'How do you survive?'

'The Tagaar give us scraps, but we also have lichen farms which supply most of our food.'

Brodie thought she had misheard the man. 'Lichen?'

'It is commonplace on Talias,' he said. 'The conditions are right to grow a particular type of lichen. It sucks nutrients from the air and grows from our waste.'

Brodie's stomach turned over at the thought, but she said nothing.

'We have learnt to work together to survive,' Ragin said. 'Some of the people here were sworn enemies before we were attacked by the Tagaar. Now we are friends.'

'So you can understand how important it is to fight the Tagaar.'

'Fighting is necessary when it is possible to win,' Ragin said. 'Unfortunately, we cannot prevail against them.'

'You said you built cannons—'

'Parts of cannons. The Tagaar would not be so foolish as to let us have control of weapons.'

They reached a building constructed from a framework of scrap metal and covered in rags. Ragin led them inside. A raised dais in the center was obviously used for speakers. Another chamber lay at the back in near darkness. They were led into the rear chamber through a thin curtain. A lamp in the middle dimly illuminated the area.

'Petitioners to the Council normally wait here

until they are heard,' Tomay said. 'I will ask you to remain here until the Council assembles.'

Brodie and the others nodded. Tomay and Regis disappeared through the curtain. No-one said anything until they left the Council Chambers.

'They can't just hand us over to the Tagaar!' Dan exploded. 'That would be murder.'

'I say we find a way out of here,' Ebony said. 'We need to get away from these crazy people.'

'They're not crazy,' Brodie said. 'They're just desperate to survive.'

'We don't even know if it's possible to escape from here,' Zena said. 'And what would happen to those who remain in Sartaria?'

'What do you mean?' Dan asked.

'Can you imagine the anger of the Tagaar if we are not handed over?' Zena continued. 'If they are prepared to kill a slave every hour—'

'Then nothing would stop them from massacring these people,' Brodie said. 'No. We can't just leave.'

'Ferdy and his friends have many advantages,'

Ferdy said.

The autistic boy had been so quiet that Brodie had completely forgotten about him. 'You mean our superpowers.'

He nodded. 'Ferdy has great strength and great intelligence, and Dan can manipulate metals, and Ebony can—'

'Thanks, Ferdy,' Brodie stopped him. 'You're right. We do have powers. A co-ordinated attack could—'

There was the sound of approaching feet from the Council area. A large assortment of aliens entered the chambers. Some of them appeared to be members of the Council, though others seemed to be carrying crude weapons. Tomay and Ragin pushed the curtain aside.

'Why are you armed?' Bax demanded. 'We are not looking for trouble.'

Tomay looked dismayed. 'I told them you were peaceful, but—'

'We make our own peace,' Ragin said. 'Now is the time for talking. After that a decision must be made.'

'The decision is easy,' a man behind them said loudly. 'The strangers must be handed over to the Tagaar.'

'You sound like a sympathiser,' a woman said. She had a fine covering of scales that glinted in the pale light. 'Since when did we start collaborating with the Fish Heads?'

'My people,' Tomay said. 'Everyone will have their say. Then the strangers may speak.'

The next half an hour passed slowly. Each of the people who spoke appeared to be from different planets. They were all humanoid in shape; they had two arms and legs and a head, but there the resemblance ended. One of them had only one eye. It was a long slit that ran across the front of his face. Another man had four eyes; two were planted on each side of his skinny, pale blue face.

Brodie had expected most of them to be in favor of simply handing them over to the Tagaar, but to her surprise there was a great deal of argument. It was obvious they all hated their alien overlords. They dearly wanted to regain their freedom, but it quickly became obvious that the residents of Sartaria were all too aware of the difficulties of escape.

Tomay finally took the podium again. 'Now we should hear from one of our visitors.'

Brodie had expected to be the one to speak, but much to her surprise, Ebony grabbed her arm.

'I'd like to do this,' she said. 'If you don't mind.'

'Be my guest,' Brodie replied.

She shook her head in some amazement as she watched Ebony walk up to the podium. It seemed like only a few months ago that Ebony had been almost unhealthily quiet. She had seemed afraid of her own shadow, but in a short time she had changed into a different person.

Go girl, Brodie thought. *You tell them.*

'Up till now you have been without weapons to defeat the Tagaar,' Ebony said. 'You have been locked in this place and worked to death. You have had your rights and your freedom taken away from you.'

'We know all this, girl,' one of the men called.

'Tell us something new,' another challenged her.

'Now you have weapons,' Ebony said.

The crowd looked at her in confusion.

'What weapons?' a woman asked.

'Us,' Ebony said.

A few of the assembled crowd looked at each other. A few of them laughed.

'You're mad, girl,' a woman in the crowd said. 'What can a group of children do?'

Ebony reached into the air. In the next instant she held what appeared to be a sword of fire. She moved it about, waving it at some of the nearest people in the crowd. Brodie watched their reaction. Even she was impressed.

'My friends and I are modified humans,' Ebony said. 'We have powers greater than a normal being.'

'Your magic tricks may impress some.' A man stepped forward. 'I am Gardan. It takes more than a flaming sword to impress me. And it will take more than a girl with magic tricks to defeat the Tagaar.'

'You sound as if you are afraid,' Ebony said.

The warrior's face went dark. 'I am not afraid. I am a soldier of Belemus. We are among the greatest warriors of the galaxy.'

'Then join us in our fight against the Tagaar,' Ebony said. 'Remaining here will only bring you death and—'

A boy came running into the tent. He whispered to one of the men.

'The Tagaar have arrived at the portal,' the man said. 'They have seized a number of citizens.'

'What is the portal?' Ebony asked.

Tomay stepped forward. 'It is the link between Sartaria and the upper ship. If they have already taken some of our people—'

'The time for talking has ended,' Regis said. 'We must decide.'

Ebony stepped down from the podium while Tomay asked for a vote to be taken. She looked despondent as she returned to the others in the petitioners' room.

'I don't think I won them over,' she said.

'You did your best,' Dan said.

'You ran out of time.' Brodie gripped her shoulder. 'A few more minutes and you would have had them.'

'We can't give up yet,' Dan said. 'They might still decide in our favour.'

'Maybe,' Ebony replied. 'If we're lucky.'

No-one said anything after that. They waited in silence while the Council of Sartaria voted on whether they should live or whether they should die.

Chapter Twenty-Three

I could not pull the trigger.

My throat was dry. My vision had a sharpness of clarity I had never before experienced. I focused on the Russian leader. The gun shook in my hand until it sagged in my grip. I had come so far. I had sacrificed so much. Brodie's life depended on me firing the weapon at the Russian Premier. Yet I could not pull the trigger. The Premier saw my hesitation.

'You are a boy,' he said. 'You do not wish to—'

'Shut up!'

It sounded like my words had been spoken by a stranger.

Alexi Kozlov clamped his mouth shut. I stood there with the gun in my hand, undecided as to what to do next. If I did not pull the trigger and immobilize the Premier, I would be condemning Brodie to death.

But I could not fire.

A sound came from behind me. I spun around to find Chad stumbling through the undergrowth. He had a bruise under his eye and a streak of blood ran down the side of his face.

'I thought I saw you land over here,' he said.

'Are you okay?'

'Peachy. I feel like I've just gone ten rounds with Rocky.' He nodded towards the Premier. 'So you haven't put the freeze on the Russian?'

'Not yet.'

'I knew you wouldn't.'

'How would—'

He stepped forward and placed a hand on my shoulder. 'Axel. You're just not the Stonekiller kind of guy.'

Tears filled my eyes. I struggled to speak. 'But Brodie—'

'We'll find another way,' he said. 'I promise.'

We stood silently in the Russian forest. 'How far away is the Flex?'

'Some distance.' He studied me. 'What are you thinking?'

'The closer we are to Graal, the closer we are to Brodie.'

'If they even bring her,' he said. 'This whole

gig with the Premier and the Stonekiller may just be a scam. Maybe he was intending to lead you on forever.'

'I know.' I shifted my eyes to the Russian Premier. He looked like he was ready to jump to his feet and attempt an escape. I hoped he wouldn't make the attempt. While I might not use the Stonekiller on him, I was more than prepared to subdue him. 'Brodie could already be dead,' I continued. 'This may have just been a big waste of time.'

'Not a complete waste of time,' he said. 'I've always wanted to see Russia. Great place for a holiday—'

'You're an idiot,' I informed him.

The Premier looked up at us as if we were crazy.

He was probably right.

We took the Russian Premier with us back to the Flex. Fortunately Chad was able to locate it in the midst of a wood several miles away. Climbing aboard, we located restraints in one of the compartments and handcuffed Alexi Kozlov to a seat in the rear. He looked none too pleased about being treated like a prisoner.

'What is this all about?' he demanded. 'Am I being held hostage?'

'Uh, yes,' I replied.

'What are you after? Money? Is this a political protest?'

'It's about those dolls,' Chad told him.

'Dolls?'

'Those Russian babushka dolls. The ones where you fit one doll inside another.'

'What about them?' The Premier looked at him in astonishment.

'They're creepy. We're holding you hostage until your government agrees to stop their manufacture—'

'Ignore him,' I told the Premier. 'We'll tell you later.'

I quickly checked his pockets, removed his cell phone and discarded it. Chad and I left Alexi alone in the rear compartment and closed the door behind us. We slumped into the pilots' seats. I felt light-headed after the events of the last twenty-four hours. I looked across at Chad and he returned my glance with a weary smile.

'Let's do Disneyland next time,' he said.

'Agreed.'

I set the autopilot. The Flex Fighter lifted up above the tree line into a clear sky. It accelerated higher and higher until the countryside was reduced to a patchwork quilt. Tension jangled at the edge of my senses. I was unsure as to what we were going to do when we met up with Graal, but for the first time in days I was feeling a little more confident.

I turned to Chad. 'Thanks for being a friend.'

He was already asleep. Probably for the best. He would not be able to accept a compliment without some snappy comeback. I examined the controls one more time and decided to join him. A few hours' sleep would—

The Flex Fighter was thrown to one side.

'Hey!' I yelled.

Chad was instantly awake. 'What's going on?'

A blast lit up the sky in front of us. A jet

fighter appeared to our right, firing another volley across our bow. I activated the computer interface.

'Computer?' I said. 'What's going on?'

'This vessel is currently being pursued by three Russian-made Sukhoi Jet Aircraft,' it informed me soberly. 'We are receiving a transmission from one of the craft.'

'Let's hear it.'

The radio crackled into life.

'American agents.' The pilot spoke almost perfect English. 'You will land your vessel, hand over the Russian Premier and surrender yourselves to authorities.'

I looked at Chad. 'What should I do?'

'Didn't you engage the cloaking device?'

I was so tired I had forgotten to activate it!

'Six more jet aircraft have joined the pursuit,' the computer said calmly. 'They are forming a blockade around Flex Fighter B-22.'

We caught sight of one of the aircraft. It seemed to be only meters above our ship. It dove towards the windscreen. The Flex dropped in response.

'They're trying to force us down,' Chad said.

'We can't let that happen.' I peered down at the console. 'Computer, show a schematic of the pursuit ships.'

A three-dimensional image hovered in mid-air above the console. The fighter planes had positioned themselves in a tight formation around us. We might be able to find a gap—but possibly not without hitting one of the other craft. We had already done enough damage for one day. I wasn't going to kill an innocent pilot for doing his duty.

'What countermeasures do we have available?' I asked the computer.

'We have a full complement of chaff, decoys and dual signal capability.'

'Dual signal?' I asked. 'What is that?'

'That information is classified.'

I looked at Chad. He shrugged. 'Don't ask me. I just stole the thing.'

Another shot was fired across the bow of our craft. It exploded ahead of us, rocking the Flex violently from side to side.

'If that's supposed to be a warning shot...' Chad stirred uncomfortably. 'They need to look up the word 'warning' in the dictionary.'

'Computer,' I said. 'On my mark, deploy a complement of chaff, engage the cloaking device and initiate the dual signal...thingy. And give me flight control of the Flex.'

Chad looked at me. 'Are you sure—'

'No.' I gripped the control stick of the aircraft. 'But I'd rather crash us than have the onboard computer do it.'

'Twelve more fighter craft are closing in on our position from the east,' the computer calmly reported. 'In addition, a group of super powered humans are approaching from the west.'

This was getting too crowded for comfort. 'Computer. Give me flight control.'

I felt the craft shudder slightly. I had flown a Flex Fighter in a lot of practice situations, but never under these circumstances. And never against a squadron of experienced pilots. The radio crackled to life again.

'American craft,' the pilot said. 'We will fire on your position if you do not immediately descend.'

Chad radioed back to them. 'Klaatu barada nikto.'

'What the hell does that mean?' I asked him.

'No idea,' he said. 'They said it on that old movie, The Day The Earth Stood Still. It sounded cool.'

'Great.' I returned my attention to the display. 'Computer, ready countermeasures.'

'Countermeasures ready.'

'On my mark...now!'

I felt the Flex shudder as chaff—a type of shrapnel normally used to give a false reading to radar—erupted from the rear. At the same time, I saw another signal on the display. It was dangerously close. Too close. It was literally on top of us.

'What's that other plane doing?' I screamed in panic. 'It's right on top of us!'

'That is the Dual Signal,' the computer intoned calmly.

I ignored it and searched the three-dimensional display for a gap. One had appeared. Slightly behind us and above—but the new ship was in its way. I gripped the control column in frustration.

Where had the other ship come from?

'It's not real!' Chad yelled. 'It's just a decoy!'

Not real—?

I ignored the image of the new ship and pulled back on the column. We flew straight through the new vessel and slipped through the gap in the surrounding fighter craft. I took us away from the mass of aircraft, rising high into the sky above them. Examining the display, I saw that most of the remaining ships were still in formation, although one of them appeared to be in severe difficulty.

'What's the status of the Russian fighter craft?' I asked the computer.

'Most of the fighter craft remain in position. One was struck by the chaff deployed from this craft,' the computer said. 'The pilot has ejected safely from the vessel.'

Thank goodness, I thought. *And the dual*

signal—

'It's a hologram,' Chad said, reading my mind. 'The fighter craft think they're still following us.'

I returned the plane to autopilot and collapsed into the seat. This was rapidly turning into the longest day of my life. I checked the timer on my wrist compass. I still had fourteen hours till I was due to meet Graal.

'Computer,' I said. 'Wake us in ten hours.'

I don't know if it replied, because I was already asleep.

Chapter Twenty-Four

'I'm sorry,' Tomay said. 'The Council has decided to hand you over to the Tagaar.'

'That's all right,' Brodie said. 'We can handle ourselves.'

Brodie felt furious, but she tried not to show her anger to the alien leader. She suspected the vote had been very close. Now they had to deal with the fallout from that decision. She asked if she could speak privately to the others for a moment. Tomay looked worried, but he nodded and left the waiting room.

'What'll we do?' Dan asked.

'We can look upon this as an advantage,' Bax said.

'Really?' Ebony replied. She felt annoyed and disappointed that her plea to the Council had been ignored. 'How is this to our advantage?'

'We wanted to leave Sartaria,' Bax said. 'Now is our chance.'

Brodie nodded. 'We can surrender and then fight back at the right moment.'

The others agreed. It seemed like the best course of action. Brodie led them into the Council Chambers. Tomay was obviously expecting a fight and he looked immediately relieved when Brodie told him to take them to the square.

They followed him through the endless shanty town of buildings. It amazed Brodie that Tomay—or anyone—could find their way through this endless labyrinth. People stopped and pointed at them as they passed. At first Brodie thought they were simply curious because they were strangers, but after a few minutes she realized many of the inhabitants were angry.

'Are they unhappy with us or—' she began.

'I think they're angry with the Council,' Ebony said.

'But if the alternative is to allow the Tagaar to execute their own citizens—'

'They hate the Tagaar. They probably consider any collaboration with them a crime.'

They finally reached an open area adjacent to the hull of the vessel. A large group had assembled and it appeared more were joining them with every passing moment. Some looked curious. Others looked downright hostile.

An enormous door, measuring about fifty feet across and twenty feet high, was built into the hull. A warning alarm started to ring and the door started to slide upward. Two Tagaar warriors, armed with assault rifles, appeared in the gap. They aimed them at the crowd. Another Tagaar warrior followed them. The bright light behind them reduced their forms to silhouettes.

Tomay stepped forward. 'We have brought the strangers!'

The crowd parted, revealing Brodie and the others.

'You are pathetic!' the third warrior yelled. 'That girl has more courage than all the slave scum living in this ghetto!'

Brodie peered at the warrior and realized it was Breel, the ship's commander. She wasn't sure if she should accept the comment as a compliment, then realized it was—in a strange way. She was trying to formulate a reply when Ebony pushed past her. The smaller girl raised her fist at the warriors.

'The Tagaar are bullies!' she yelled. 'You have no honor! You lie and you cheat!'

The three warriors leveled their weapons at the petite girl. 'You will be sorry, child!' Breel snapped. 'We'll reduce your planet to a cinder that will float—'

Brodie's memory of the next few seconds would forever remain a blur. Whatever Breel had wanted to say would forever remain a mystery because Ebony chose that moment to attack. Within seconds she had crossed the area in a sprint, transmuting two machete knives in mid-air. The two soldiers on either side of the commander were completely taken by surprise; obviously no-one had stood up to them for so long they had forgotten what resistance looked like. Ebony struck down Breel with a double blow.

'Revolution!' she cried. 'Revolution!'

One of the warriors fired ineffectively into the deck. The other stumbled backward. Brodie was so amazed she didn't know what to say, but Dan took up the cry immediately.

'Revolution!' he yelled. 'Down with the Tagaar!'

'Freedom!' someone in the crowd yelled.

'Kill the Tagaar!' another voice rang out.

Ebony dove to one side as the Tagaar warriors recovered. They opened fire on the crowd. People screamed and ducked for cover. Some people were hit. Dan focused on a piece of sheet metal on one of the makeshift roofs. It flew through the air and struck one of the warriors, killing him immediately.

The remaining warrior continued to fire as he withdrew through the door. Ebony climbed to her feet.

'Revolution!' she yelled.

A hundred voices had already taken up the cry. Several other people were cheering at the death of Breel and the warrior. Brodie and her friends caught up to Ebony. Dan slapped her on the back.

'You're amazing!' he said.

'Not really.' The girl blushed in the pale light.

'I just don't like bullies.'

Zena appeared at their side. 'We've got to press the advantage,' she said. 'With this many people we may be able to take over the ship.'

They started forward, but the door had started to slide shut. Dan focused on it and buckled it out of shape. It ground to a halt. By now they could hear a chant of voices ringing behind them. The revolt seemed to have spread across the length and breadth of Sartaria within seconds. It seemed the whole society had been like a powder keg waiting to explode. All it needed was a match—and Ebony had provided it.

'Well done, girl,' Brodie said as they started up the corridor.

'Thanks,' she said. 'Now we just need to take over the ship.'

It immediately became obvious that this was going to be easier said than done. The single guard at the far end of the corridor was joined by another group of warriors. Ebony formed a shield and Ferdy wielded it before them as the aliens began firing at them. Brodie looked back and saw a multitude of people starting down the tunnel with makeshift weapons. Most of the weapons looked like they were tools used for metal working.

'Anyone got any ideas?' she asked.

Ebony turned to Dan. 'You remember the baseball manoeuvre?'

'Do I ever?' Dan smiled. 'Bat 'er up.'

Ebony focused on the air before the shield and created a steel ball. Dan sent it flying towards the approaching troops. They heard a scream and the sound of running. Ebony and Dan repeated the procedure half a dozen times.

'Ferdy does not like it when we hurt people,' Ferdy said. 'But we have to fight back if people shoot at Ferdy and his friends.'

'Absolutely,' Ebony agreed.

'In 455AD,' Ferdy continued, 'Roman Emperor Petronius Maximus was stoned to death by an angry mob after only seventy-eight days on the throne.'

'Uh, I didn't know that.' Ebony raised an

eyebrow. 'I don't think we'll be meeting him today.'

'Obviously, friend Ebony.' Ferdy looked at her as if she were dumb. 'He is dead.'

'Thanks for clearing that up.'

Brodie looked past them up the corridor. The Tagaar were nowhere to be seen. She urged the others forward until they reached another door. By now the corridor was very full of people. Brodie was sure they had a good chance of taking over the entire ship if they could access a store of weapons.

'Ferdy,' Brodie said. 'We need firepower for these people. Are you able to hack into the Tagaar communications system?'

'I can.'

He smiled at her.

'Uh, will you do it, please?' Brodie asked.

'Of course.' He laid down the enormous metal shield. Pulling open a nearby panel, he manipulated the wires for a moment. A series of hieroglyphics appeared on a small computer screen. After a few minutes he drew back from the panel, frowned and punched a few more buttons.

'How are you doing?' Brodie asked.

'Ferdy is well.'

'Have you succeeded in hacking the system?'

'Not yet,' he replied. 'Ferdy first had to learn the Tagaar language and counting system. The language contains almost a million words while the Tagaar use a Base-12 numeric system.'

'Oh.'

Ferdy continued to punch buttons on the panel. He made a satisfied sound after another minute. 'There is a weapons storage area one hundred meters to our left and one floor up.'

Brodie examined the wall. 'This looks pretty thick. Maybe we should—'

Ferdy punched a hole straight through the metal, revealing the room beyond. He tore a jagged gap in the wall so large that two people could fit through at a time.

'It is not so thick,' he said. 'See?'

Chapter Twenty-Five

I was awakened by the sound of a droning alarm. Opening my eyes with difficulty, I tried to bring myself back into wakefulness. I saw a view screen and a control panel. Chad was sound asleep in the pilot's seat next to me.

Where was I?

I can't say it all came flooding back to me. I'd been through too much over the last couple of days for that to occur. Instead, my memories returned in a piecemeal fashion. Last of all I remembered that the Premier of Russia—Alexi Kozlov—was handcuffed to a seat in the back of the Flex Fighter.

Oh hell. How had I gotten myself into this mess?

The alarm continued to sound. I turned my focus to the control panel. A light was flashing.

'Holy hell,' I muttered. 'Computer. What is the source of the alarm?'

'Main power has dropped to ten percent.'

'Why has the power suddenly dropped?'

'Power loss is due to normal consumption.'

Normal consumption? This was weird. One of the staff at The Agency had told me the power supply for one of these would last for years.

'What's using the power?' I asked.

'Life support, engines…' The computer's voice droned on, listing a multitude of ship wide systems. Then it said something that caught my attention.

'Computer, what was that last item?'

'Power drainage from the outer hull.'

'What is that?'

'A device is attached to the outer hull that is draining energy at ten times normal rate.'

I wasn't sure what it was, but the Russians must have fired something at us before we escaped. I pushed Chad half a dozen times before he finally woke up.

'What's going on?' he asked.

'We have to put down for a while.'

'Why?'

I explained the problem regarding the hull.

'Yeah,' he said. 'Put us down anywhere.'

He promptly went back to sleep.

'Computer,' I said. 'Bring us in to land.'

'Confirmed.'

I heard a slight rev of the engines and the vessel dipped. I looked at the countdown on the wrist compass. I still had six hours till I was due to meet Graal. I still had not formulated a plan as to how to save Brodie—assuming she was still alive—but at least I did not feel quite so alone. I watched the landscape draw closer by the moment. We dipped low over some trees and found a glade in the middle of a forest.

'Computer,' I said. 'Where are we?'

'Current position is approximately fifty miles west of the Gouin Reseroir.'

'Uh…where is that?'

'The Province of Quebec.'

Canada, I thought. *Not quite the way I wanted to visit this wonderful country.*

The Flex gently set down.

Chad stirred. 'Are we there yet?'

'Come on. I need your help.'

'Doing what?'

I groaned and explained again about the device attached to the hull. He stretched and half fell out of the pilot's seat. We entered to the rear section of the vessel and found the Premier wide awake. Obviously he was too worried to sleep.

'What are we doing?' he asked. 'Is a ransom to be paid?'

'There's not going to be any ransom,' I said.

The man immediately looked alarmed.

'No, I mean—' I wasn't sure how to explain this. 'I'm sorry you've been dragged into this. There's a hostage situation taking place and we need your help.'

'Is there to be a prisoner exchange?' he asked.

'Uh, something like that.'

'That's right.' Chad shook his head unhappily. 'We're trading you for a shipment of babushka dolls. I warned you—'

'Ignore him,' I instructed the Premier. 'We'll be back in a minute.'

I practically dragged Chad through the back

door of the ship. We found ourselves in the middle of a clearing surrounded by tall trees. Chad and I began examining the outside of the ship. After a minute we found a device the size of a plate attached to the side.

'This doesn't look normal,' Chad said.

We pried it free and Chad used his flame power to melt it into slag.

'Let's just hope that wasn't part of the engine,' I said.

'I doubt it.' He glanced up into the surrounding forest. 'I'm getting that weird feeling.'

'Indigestion?'

'No.' He peered through the network of trees. 'Like we're being watched.'

I stared into the forest. It looked completely deserted.

Still...

'Let's get moving,' I said. 'The sooner—'

A voice boomed from the undergrowth. 'This is Canadian Special Forces. Get down on the ground. Place your hands on the back of your head. Do not move.'

Hell.

Chad and I started around the side of the vessel, but at the same moment someone—or something—flew straight out of the forest and slammed into both of us. It was like being hit by a cannonball. We went sprawling across the ground as the shape disappeared out of sight. I tried standing, but I had been winded. Chad was faster on his feet. He started erecting an ice wall around the perimeter. It had reached a height of about six feet when the second attack happened.

A blast of purple energy smashed a hole in the wall. By now I was back on my feet again, but the beam of light slammed into me and I went flying once more. I groaned. A hail of bullets hit the wall, reducing it to icy rubble. I tried rising again, but something knocked me to the ground for the third time.

I rolled over. The figure standing above me was the human cannonball that had crashed into me. I struggled to my knees as he drew back a fist.

'I'm Tasker,' he said. 'Time to say

goodnight.'

He slammed his fist into my jaw and darkness swallowed me.

Chapter Twenty-Six

The rain had stopped.

Morgan Le Fay sipped at her cup of tea as she peered through the window of the small cottage. There were few things she would miss when she left Earth, but a good cup of tea was one of them. She always took hers with sugar and cream. A small pastry on the side never went astray either. It was a shame this cottage was so ill-equipped to satisfy her, but sometimes she was forced to settle for second best.

She sighed. The view from the cottage was delightful. From here she could watch the sea and the mighty heaving waves off the coast. A lovely view. Still, there would be many stimulating vistas awaiting her once she acquired the necessary technology to leave this world. A muffled groan came from behind her. She glanced back at the owners of the cottage. An elderly couple named George and Sarah Bell stood with their adult son, Bruce, like toy soldiers at attention. Morgan placed down her cup of tea. Inclining her head to the elderly woman, she said,

'You may speak.'

The woman gasped and let out a low cry. Despite the return of her power of speech, it still took the old woman a moment to form words.

'Who are you?' she gasped. 'What are you? What do you—'

Morgan gave a small wave of her hand and silenced the woman again. 'So many questions. I can see why I shut you up in the first place.' She took another sip of her tea. Drumming her fingers on the table, she decided to try the son.

'Young man,' she said. 'I am going to ask you some questions.'

She allowed him to speak. Instead of being grateful for the return of his voice, his face convulsed with hatred. 'Release us!' he yelled. 'What sort of monster—'

'I will be the one asking the questions,' Morgan said. She was beginning to tire of these people. She flicked a wrist and the son abruptly turned and punched his mother in the face. The old woman's head snapped to one side, but she remained standing.

'You will cause your mother pain every time you do not answer me,' Morgan instructed him. 'Do you understand?'

Bruce Bell was a big man—well over six feet in height—but now he cried like a baby.

'Yes…yes, I understand.'

'Now, I want to know about The Solar Accelerator,' Morgan said. 'What security is at the installation?'

'Se-security?'

'Yes, you oaf!' Morgan snapped. 'Security!'

'Well…they have a lot of security.' Bruce's eyes were moving about wildly in his head. 'They have police and the army and guns…'

'Oh, you stupid boy.' Morgan tut-tutted him. 'I hate it when people lie to me. I really do. And people who lie to me must be punished.'

She spent the next hour exacting punishment on the helpless family. The elderly couple were close to death by the time Morgan had finished. Finally she allowed Bruce to speak again and he immediately burst into tears.

'Stop whining,' she snapped. 'Now tell me about the security at the installation.'

'There isn't any,' he sobbed. 'It's a research facility.'

'What about cameras?'

'I...I don't know,' he said. 'I don't think there are any.'

Morgan nodded. It was just as she suspected. While being immortal, she was not impervious to harm; she could be killed by a bullet in the same manner as anyone else. She had not lived this long without being cautious.

'I believe you're telling me the truth,' she said. 'And how many scientists work at the array?'

'A-about half a dozen.'

'Good...good,' she mused. 'Well, I think that just about covers it, but I have one last question.'

'Please,' Bruce begged. 'My parents...they need medical help...'

Morgan shut him up. She would have to do this herself. She finished her tea—it had gone cold because of that stupid boy—and began a thorough search of the house. Finally she found what she was seeking in a back room of the small cottage.

Paraffin.

Wonderful, she thought. *A fire on a cold afternoon is so pleasant.*

She handed the tin to Bruce and made him splash it throughout the house. Finally Morgan forced him to pour the remaining liquid over his parents and himself. Morgan rooted through a set of drawers until she found what she was seeking.

A lighter.

She offered it to Bruce. The young man struggled against her. She could see him exerting every bit of willpower to stop himself from raising his hand, but finally it jerked into place and he gripped the lighter tightly.

'Good.' Morgan cast a last glance about the small living area. 'Now that looks rather nice.'

A shawl lay across the back of one of the chairs.

'I do believe this is alpaca hair.' She fondled it

gently. 'It's lovely. Too good to burn.'

Morgan went to the door of the cottage and opened it wide. Gray clouds scudded across the sky. It had grown even colder and she was immensely pleased she had taken the shawl. She wrapped it around her, closed the door and headed up the street. At the top of the hill lay the Solar Accelerator. It was an imposing structure; a large concrete building with a huge antenna pointed skyward. After a moment she gave a flick of her hand. An enormous *swoosh*, followed by a single cry, emanated from the cottage behind her.

She continued up the hill.

Chapter Twenty-Seven

I awoke slowly.

I was in a moving vehicle. An aircraft. Lifting my head slowly, I realized I was on a bench with Chad sitting next to me. He was already awake. He looked both scared and angry. Opposite us sat the man named Tasker and two army personnel. One had red hair. The other was blonde. To my left, I could see the pilots at the front of the ship. We were in a vessel not dissimilar in design to the Flex Fighter. Possibly it was a little smaller.

I tried to open my mouth. My jaw hurt like hell.

'Sorry about that punch, kid.' Tasker smirked. 'I don't know my own strength sometimes.'

I looked down at my handcuffs. They were attached to a chain set into the floor. I tried using my powers to break the cuffs apart.

'You're wasting your time,' Tasker said, glancing up at the roof.

I followed his gaze. Two zeno emitters were set into the ceiling. They produced a dampening field that nullified our powers completely.

'Who are you people?' I asked. 'You're not Canadian Special Forces.'

He laughed. 'You're right about that,' he said. 'We're a group known as Stint. We're mercenaries. Someone hired us to take you out, and we did.'

'Where's Alexi Kozlov?'

'In the other Lifter.'

'Lifter?'

'It's like that clever little ship you boys were flying around in.' He leant forward. 'I've got to hand it to you. That was quite a heist you pulled off.'

'Heist?'

'The Russian Premier!' He shook his head in admiration. 'You're all over the news. The United States and Russia are ready to start firing nukes at each other.'

'I'm sorry.'

'I bet you are.' He obviously didn't believe my expression of remorse. 'Can I ask you a question?'

'You can ask.'

'Why did you do it?' he asked. 'Was it for money?'

'My girlfriend's being held hostage,' I said. 'Look, the world is in real danger. If I don't—'

'Danger?' Tasker laughed. 'I'll say. The US is at Defcon Two. We might all be eating radioactive burgers for dinner.'

'The Russian Premier—'

'Don't you worry about him. He's absolutely fine, and we intend to keep him that way. He's just the icing on the cake. A bonus.'

'What do you mean?'

'Let's just say we have some contacts that will buy him from us,' Tasker explained. 'They'll resell him back to the Russians.'

'Buy?' I said in amazement. 'Sell?'

'Sure,' he said. 'Stint don't do hostage negotiations. We don't have the contacts, but we'll pass him onto someone else who does.'

'And what about us?'

Tasker looked uncomfortable. 'Yeah, that's a shame,' he said. 'Someone paid us good money to take you down. They want to do some crazy experiments on you. Take you apart to see what makes you tick.'

'Tick?' My voice went up a notch.

'You're probably not gonna survive it.' Tasker shook his head regretfully. 'Sorry. It's nothing personal. It's just business.'

I struggled to put all this together. These people were mercenaries who had kidnapped us at the behest of someone else. They had nothing to do with our kidnapping of Alexi Kozlov. He just happened to be in the wrong place at the wrong time.

Hell, I thought. *I've really made a mess of this.*

Could things get any worse? I should have gone to Agent Palmer in the first place. The Agency would have helped me. Because of the way I had handled this, Chad and I were in this alone.

'Don't look so glum,' Tasker said. 'It's an eat-or-be-eaten kind of world.'

'That makes me feel a whole lot better.'

The mercenary got up and crossed to the

pilots. He asked them about the flight plan. I looked at each of the two guards opposite. They didn't look pleasant. I desperately tried to think of some way out of this. Nothing sprang to mind.

'You kids aren't so tough without your powers.' The blonde one looked like he had trodden on something unpleasant in the street. 'You wouldn't last a minute in a real fight.'

Then he spat. On me.

'You—' I started forward to hit him, but the chain stopped short.

The redhead laughed at my desperate attempts to break free. 'You modifieds look good, but you've got no real staying power.'

Chad groaned. 'My head…'

I looked over at him. He had not spoken the entire time I had been conversing with Tasker. Now his eyes fluttered about wildly.

'Are you okay?' I asked.

'My head…can't think straight…'

He sagged so far forward his head almost touched the floor. I yelled. Tasker walked back towards us. The other two guards were still laughing, but Tasker looked serious.

'We don't want that kid dead,' he snapped at the other men. 'He's not worth anything dead.'

He pulled Chad's body back into an upright position. Much to everyone's amazement, Chad's eyes were wide open and he had a small gun in his hand.

'Surprise,' he said.

He fired the weapon and shot out the two zeno emitters. He tried shooting Tasker, but the man was too fast. The older man knocked the gun from his hand and drew back his fist. I focused on the air within the vessel and blasted the rear doors open. Exerting pressure on the floor of the cabin, I pushed the back of the vessel down.

The blonde guard fell out through the rear. Tasker brought his fist down to slam it into Chad's head, but by now I had an invisible barrier up. He hit the barrier. Recoiled in pain. Chad focused and an instant later the man fell sideways to the floor—encased in ice. The redheaded guard fired his weapon, but by now the bullets were simply bouncing off my barrier. The craft leveled out.

'Let's get out of here,' I yelled. The aircraft was filled with a hurricane of freezing cold air. I broke the handcuffs and they clattered to the ground.

Chad pointed menacingly at the other guard. 'Where's the other Lifter?'

The redheaded guard looked petrified. He pointed vaguely out through the rear of our craft. I could see a small vessel trailing us several hundred feet below.

One of the pilots turned around in his seat with a gun in his hand. Chad directed a blast of fire at him. The man screamed and the entire front window exploded outward. I felt a tinge of sympathy for the man, but there was no time to reflect.

'Come on!' I yelled.

The block of ice encasing Tasker shattered. Shards of ice flew in all directions. Chad threw up an ice wall. I knew that would only hold for a couple of seconds at most. I glanced towards the front of the craft and saw the remaining pilot desperately trying to get the ship under control. He was fighting a losing battle. Through the shattered windscreen I could see the landscape drawing closer with every passing second.

We were about to crash.

Chapter Twenty-Eight

Brodie sometimes had to remind herself that Ferdy had a multitude of abilities. Not only was he a genius, but he had super strength. She watched in amazement as he leapt from a standing position straight into the ceiling. Hanging by one hand, he tore a hole in the roof and climbed through. He reappeared a moment later.

'Ferdy has found guns,' he said. 'Lots of guns.'

'That's great, Ferdy,' Brodie said. 'We'll come up and join you.'

The chamber they were standing in was becoming more crowded by the second. It seemed the entire population of Sartaria had decided to participate in the impromptu revolution and had escaped the vast slave city in one enormous wave. The room was some sort of large supply chamber filled with boxes. Someone had broken one open and found food supplies. They had begun to distribute them to the crowd while Brodie and the others stacked a few boxes and used them to climb up into the room above. It quickly became apparent that Ferdy had discovered the mother lode. It was more than a storage chamber. It was a full armory. There were hundreds of rifles lining the walls. People started up the makeshift ladder after them.

Brodie realized they needed a plan and they needed it quickly.

'We need to take command of the bridge,' Zena said. It turned out she had been a military officer on Corrida. 'Once we have control of this ship we can go wherever we want.'

'How do we get there?' Bax asked.

Ferdy brought up a schematic on the wall displaying a diagram of the ship. While Bax and Zena studied it, Brodie assembled her friends. The last few hours had been so chaotic it seemed a million years since they had been able to speak.

'How is everyone holding up?' she asked.

'I'm fine,' Dan said. 'I'm part of a rebellion taking place on an alien ship orbiting the Earth. What more could a boy want?'

The group laughed.

'I'm okay,' Ebony said. 'A little tired, but still on my feet.'

'What about you, Ferdy?' Brodie asked.

'Ferdy is having fun,' he said.

'Fun?' Dan said.

'Ferdy likes to be with his friends.' The boy placed his arms around them and they all huddled closer together. 'We will meet later with our friends Chad and Axel. We will play some games.'

'I'm sure we will,' Brodie said.

The mention of Axel's name made Brodie realize how much she missed him. During the last few, crazy hours she had not had a chance to think about him. He had been sent on a mission by the Tagaar to create disharmony. What did that mean? Was he all right? Was he even alive?

She wondered sometimes about her feelings for him. He had never used the L word. What did that mean? Maybe they weren't in love. Maybe they were just friends. Certainly, he often seemed preoccupied with his own thoughts. She had noticed he spent a lot of time with Ebony. Maybe that meant—

She stopped herself.

Shut up, she thought. *And focus!*

Bax and Zena rejoined them.

'We have a plan,' Bax said. 'We will make our way through the ship until we reach Engineering.'

'Why Engineering?' Ebony asked.

Zena spoke. 'If we control the power supply, we control the ship.'

'Then we need to advance.' The voice came from behind them. It was Ragin. 'You should know that I regret my previous actions. I can see we should not have agreed to hand you over to the Tagaar.'

'Don't blame yourself,' Brodie said. 'You were doing what you felt was right for your people.'

'I think we need to keep moving,' Dan said. 'This room is getting pretty full.'

He was right. The surge of people from Sartaria had not slowed. The armory was almost full to overflowing. More and more people were streaming up the makeshift ladder into the room with every passing second.

Zena yelled a few commands to several of the

armed citizens. Someone carefully opened the door leading to the corridor beyond. It was deserted. The crowd swelled through the gap and started pouring down the corridor. Brodie found herself being carried along with it. She caught sight of Ebony and grabbed the girl's arm.

'Stay close,' she said. 'I'm not sure if this is such a good idea.'

'What do you mean?' Ebony asked.

'There are too many people,' Brodie said. 'We need to—'

At that moment she saw the light above the elevator flash at the far end of the corridor. A cry went up among the people and several armed resistance fighters readied their guns to fire. The doors opened to reveal—nothing.

'What's going on?' Dan asked. He was shorter than the others and could not see over the sea of heads.

'It is empty, Dan,' Ferdy said.

The crowd continued to drive them forward.

'We need to stop,' Ebony said, feeling

claustrophobic in the confined area. She turned around to yell. 'Stop! Everyone stop!'

At the same moment, Brodie saw someone step into the elevator. There was a sudden flash and then bodies and pieces of metal were flying towards them. The shockwave of an explosion followed. Brodie felt the impact of the blast hit her and throw her sideways. Everything went dark for a few seconds. When she opened her eyes she realized she was on the ground, surrounded by bloodied and screaming people. She struggled to her feet and saw Dan.

'What happened?' he asked. The boy had a mixture of tears, blood and mucus on his face.

'It was a bomb.' Brodie's ears were still ringing. 'A trap.'

People were all over the ground and all over each other in the confined space of the corridor. Screams and crying emanated from every direction. Blood covered the floor. It seemed everywhere Brodie looked, she saw death and pain.

'We need people with medical knowledge!'

she screamed. 'We need doctors! Please, we—'

Ebony grabbed her arm. 'Breathe,' she said. 'Just try to breathe.'

Brodie realized she was on the verge of hysteria. And only barely conscious. The world shifted around her and she fell back into Ebony's arms. She realized she was staring up at the ceiling. Someone moved past her field of vision. It was Tomay. He looked down at her.

'Are you all right?' he asked. 'The blast has killed many people, but—'

Brodie forced herself out of Ebony's arms. She gave her friend a grateful look and struggled back to her feet. Somehow, medical care was being given to the victims of the blast. People were still working together in the midst of the carnage. The people of Sartaria were amazing.

'I'm okay.' She searched for Bax. The woman had survived the blast unharmed, although she was covered in someone's blood. Brodie stumbled over the field of bodies to her.

'It was a bomb,' Bax said. 'A trap laid by the

Tagaar.'

'I thought so,' Brodie said. 'Where's Zena?'

Bax's face fell. 'Zena is dead. She was directly in the path of the blast. She was trying to stop them from entering the elevator, but—' The woman's face threatened to crumple into tears. 'Anyway, we must regroup. We must continue.'

At that moment an alarm began to sound in the corridor. It stopped after several seconds and was replaced by a growling voice.

'This is Commander Graal,' it said.

The moaning and crying in the corridor subsided enough for them to be able to hear his voice.

'I have taken command of this ship,' he continued. 'You will return to the lower decks. You will be treated fairly if you resume your work.'

'And if we don't?' Bax asked.

The commander's next words could have almost been in response to her question.

'You will return within the hour,' Graal continued. 'If you do not we will kill every slave aboard this vessel.'

Chapter Twenty-Nine

I grabbed Chad's arm. I was so disoriented by our journey towards the ground that I dared not try to save the vessel. Forming an invisible barrier, I aimed it at the nearest wall. At the same instant Tasker started towards us. Dragging Chad out of his path, I flew us towards the gap. One second we were in the heart of the twisting, out of control vessel. In the next we were out in the freezing cold air and soaring into the sky.

I peered back to see the Lifter slam into the ground. A roar of flame erupted from the ship. I tried not to think of the men aboard the craft. We landed among a clump of trees a short distance away.

'You did good, Axel,' he said.

'Thanks.' I was still thinking of the men aboard the jet. 'Do you think anyone got out?'

'Who cares?' His face hardened. 'They were going to use us for medical experiments.'

'Who do you think was behind it?'

'No idea.' He shook his head. 'Just another weirdo.'

Another thought occurred tome. 'And where did you get that gun? Since when did you start…'

'Packing?' he laughed. 'You know how many times we've been taken down by those zeno emitters?'

'Lots?'

'Dan helped me with his Jedi powers to buy it from a pawnbroker in downtown Vegas. I thought it might come in handy.'

Peering into the sky, I could just make out a tiny dot in the sea of blue. 'We've got to get going.'

'How are we doing for time?'

My eyes shot to the display on the wrist compass. I stared at it in horror, unable to make a sound. I could not believe my eyes.

0:00

We had been unconscious for a lot longer than I realized. More than six hours. The rendezvous time had come—and gone. Chad grabbed my arm as I reeled on my feet.

'You did your best, man,' he said. 'You risked everything for her.'

'I know.'

Brodie was dead. I could not even conceive of it. I did not feel hatred or anger. Only shock. An all-consuming numbness.

'Axel?' Chad's voice came from a million miles away. 'There's still the Russian Premier.'

Alexi Kozlov? Of course. I had dragged him into this mess. Now I had to get him out of it.

'I'd better move,' I said.

'It looks like the Lifter was using some sort of tractor beam to tow our Flex behind it,' Chad said. 'I saw it crash into the woods as we came into land.'

'Do you think you can find it?'

He nodded. I rose up into the air without another word and sighted the second Lifter. It was an amazing vessel, but it didn't have the speed of one of our Flex Fighters. Before long I had almost caught up with it. Drawing near, something erupted from the rear of the craft.

A missile.

I fired an invisible projectile at it and the device exploded in mid-air. Its remains tumbled to the ground. More missiles fired from the vessel and I spent the next few minutes destroying them as I closed in on the aircraft. Finally I damaged one of the wings and the vessel went into a slow dive. I placed a platform under it and gently lowered it towards earth. It looked like they had either run out of missiles or motivation because no more weaponry erupted from the craft.

Landing several feet away from the craft, I heard footsteps behind me.

'I found the Flex,' Chad said. 'It's ready when we are.'

We cautiously approached the downed vessel.

'Don't forget about that other mod who was with them,' I said.

'You mean the guy with the energy beam?'

Almost in response, the rear doors of the vessel were blown outward. Chad and I dove to one side as a beam of purple energy cut through the air.

'That's who you mean?' Chad asked.

'That's him.'

I threw up an air shield and hoped it would

work. Jumping to my feet, I started forward as Purple's energy beam slammed into my shield. It held, but the impact still threw me backward into the undergrowth.

Chad fired a barrage of icy cannonballs straight at Purple, but he simply blasted them out of the air. Chad ducked and hit the ground next to me as the energy beam cut through the air again.

'We need a plan,' I said.

A moment later Chad retreated into the forest behind us as I stood up again and threw a mini-hurricane at Purple. He staggered and fell, but quickly retaliated with that beam of his. This time I stood my ground and increased my shield strength. I slowly advanced as he redoubled his efforts. Within seconds I found myself struggling against a purple haze of light and energy.

I couldn't keep this up much longer. If Chad didn't move in soon—

The energy beam died.

It took a number of seconds for my eyes to clear, but I realized Purple had not moved; now he was completely encased in a block of ice. Chad was advancing on the rear of the Lifter. I opened my mouth to yell a warning to Chad, but at that instant gunfire broke out.

Chad fell.

No.

No!

Racing forward, I threw a series of invisible cannonballs into the rear of the craft as well as a blast of hurricane air. By the time I was finished, the vessel lay on its side. A single gunman leapt from the back and fired a few times, but I took him down with a single shot of air. I turned back to where Chad had fallen. To my amazement he was on his feet and laughing.

'Worried?' he asked.

'No,' I said. 'A couple of holes in you would let out some of that hot air.'

He laughed again. We made our way to the rear of the Lifter. At the same time we heard a racket from the front of the vessel. We saw a group of three men scrambling through the shattered front window.

They raced across the clearing and disappeared into the forest.

Alexi Kozlov was alive and well. And still handcuffed to the floor of the craft. He looked at us with an expression of intense hatred.

'I'm glad to see you're all right, Mr. Kozlov,' I said.

'You Americans are insane,' he said.

'Hey,' Chad protested. 'I'm not American.'

'Let's not get into that now,' I said. 'We need to get moving.'

We freed Alexi and helped him from the rear of the vessel.

'What are you doing with me?' he asked. 'When will this insanity end?'

That was a good question. We had reached a turning point. I had missed the meeting with Graal. He had made himself clear that Brodie would be killed if I did not use the Stonekiller weapon on the Premier and deliver him on time. It was impossible to contact the alien. I was standing in a forest in the middle of nowhere with Chad and the Premier of

Russia. It was time to face facts.

'Axel?' Chad peered at me.

'It's over,' I told him. 'I've failed Brodie completely.'

Chapter Thirty

'It's not over yet,' Brodie said. 'Not by a long shot.'

The floor of the corridor was covered in blood and broken bodies. Smoke from the explosion filled the air. First aid was being administered to the injured. Those who had been hurt by the blast and could still move were stumbling back through the mass of people to the rear.

Yet at the same time, Brodie felt a determination in the air. Everyone was working together. Graal's announcement that everyone should simply return to the slave city below had been greeted by silence at first, but within minutes angry shouts had begun to erupt throughout the crowd.

They're not giving up, Brodie realized. *We've got to keep moving forward.*

Tomay was at her side. He looked pale and confused.

Brodie gripped his arm. 'Our plan was to reach the engine room. That hasn't changed.'

'But the explosion—'

'People have been killed,' Brodie said. 'But everyone will die if you return to Sartaria. It won't happen all at once. It might take years. But you need to make a decision. Do you want to live as a free man? Or do you want to die as a slave?'

Bax joined her. 'She's right, Tomay. The only path to take is forward.'

'But how—'

'My friends and I will make for Engineering,' Brodie said. 'We will signal you when we've taken it.'

By now Dan, Ferdy and Ebony had joined them. Tomay looked at them critically.

'I know you have powers,' he said. 'But can you do this alone?'

Ebony spoke. 'Sometimes a smaller force can do more than an entire army.'

Tomay slowly nodded. 'Then I'm going with you. The time for waiting has ended. We will either live or die today, but we'll do it as free men and women. Not as slaves.'

'And I will join you,' Bax said.

'Okay,' Brodie said. 'This is what I like to hear.'

Ferdy brought up a schematic of the ship on one of the wall displays. They examined it closely. Engineering lay at the heart of the ship. It was only two levels up and about five hundred meters from their current position.

'There is a Backup Engineering Section,' Ferdy pointed out. 'Possibly the Tagaar will switch to the backup supply.'

'Not if we're fast enough,' Tomay said.

They made their way down the corridor to the remains of the elevator. There wasn't much left. It looked like it had operated via some form of gravity propulsion as there didn't seem to be any cables in the shaft. Brodie peered upward. She could see the doors leading to the levels above.

'First we need to get up the elevator shaft,' Ebony said.

'Ferdy can do that,' Ferdy said. 'Ferdy likes to climb.'

'Are you sure?' Dan asked.

Ferdy did not wait for an answer. He jumped across the gap and grasped the framework encasing the elevator shaft. Without pausing, he started ascending. Dan found himself looking downward. The shaft seemed to continue on forever.

'That's a long way down,' he said. 'I wouldn't like to fall.'

'Don't even think about it,' Brodie said.

She looked up the shaft and saw that Ferdy had rapidly ascended. He was almost at the second level.

'Wait there!' she called. 'I'll climb up after you!'

'Ferdy is fine,' he replied. 'Ferdy will take care of everything.'

Brodie was worried.

'There is one thing.' Ferdy's voice reverberated down the shaft.

'Yes?'

'The largest city in Brazil is San Paulo.'

'That's great, Ferdy.'

They peered anxiously up the shaft, watching

Ferdy punch through one of the doors on the upper level. They heard cries and yelling and the firing of weapons. And silence.

'I'm going up there,' Brodie said. 'I never should have let him—'

A Tagaar warrior fell past them and down the seemingly bottomless elevator shaft. Two others followed him in quick succession. Nothing happened for a long moment. Brodie and the others leant back into the shaft.

Ferdy's head appeared from high above.

'The way is clear,' he called.

A moment later Ferdy dropped what appeared to be some sort of electrical conduit down the shaft and they ascended to the upper level. Dan was the last to arrive. He looked back down into the darkness of the shaft. And gulped.

'The Tagaar warriors are bad,' Ferdy told them. 'They tried to hurt Ferdy, but Ferdy hurt them instead.'

'I'm glad you're our friend,' Dan said.

Ferdy grasped his arm. 'Friends are important.

Ferdy is lucky to have such good friends.'

'I feel the same.'

'Soon Ferdy will speak to his friends Chad and Axel. Ferdy misses them.'

'We'll see them once we return to Earth.'

'Ferdy can speak to them now.'

'Uh, howzat?'

'Ferdy has calculated there is a seventy-three percent chance that Chad has made use of a modified Flex Fighter he kept hidden in the desert close to The Agency compound.'

This was all news to Dan. As they made their way down the corridor, he asked Ferdy to explain. By the time they had reached the main generator room, Dan thought he finally understood what Ferdy was saying.

'But how will we contact them?' Dan asked. 'We don't have a cell phone or a radio—'

'Ferdy can break into the Tagaar communications system and ring our friends,' he said. 'It will be fun to speak to them.'

'Right.' Dan wondered if Ferdy had

completely lost his mind. 'You can just ring them up for a chat.'

'A chat.' Ferdy nodded. 'A chat will be fun.'

They assembled around the door leading to Engineering. They expected opposition, but to their surprise they encountered no-one. It looked like the entire force of Tagaar warriors had been moved to another section of the ship.

Let's hope they're out to lunch, Brodie thought.

She had been formulating a plan. Now she outlined it to the others. It involved breaking into two groups and co-ordinating two separate assaults on the chamber beyond. The others listened in silence. They readied their weapons and pushed through the doors.

The main chamber was filled with an enormous cylindrical generator and other equipment. Brodie glanced at it. She didn't know how a normal generator on Earth worked, let alone one on an alien spaceship designed to propel it around the galaxy. However, it seemed two things were immediately obvious; the generator was not operational, and not a single Tagaar warrior was in sight.

'This was not what I expected.' Brodie turned to Tomay.

'This doesn't make any sense,' the man responded. 'The entire ship is powered by the generators.'

'Maybe they've already moved to the backup,' Bax suggested.

She brought up a schematic on the computer system. After a moment she looked at them in dismay.

'I was right. These engines have already been disabled.'

The others joined them just in time to hear her speaking.

'And the whole Tagaar army has run off,' Dan said.

'I doubt that's the case,' Tomay said. 'They are probably working out how to recapture us.'

An alarm started to sound. They looked at each other in confusion as it reverberated around the massive chamber.

'What is that?' Ebony asked.

Bax quickly examined the computer system.

'Oh no,' she said.

'What is it?' Brodie asked. 'What's that alarm?'

'It's the separation alarm,' Bax said. 'It means the main ship is separating from the lower section.'

'Separating?' Brodie repeated the word dumbly.

'This ship is able to disconnect into pieces. The lower decks form a hull distinct from the remainder of the ship. When the hull separates—'

'What will happen?' Brodie interrupted.

'We are very close to your planet,' Bax said. 'We will fall towards your world and burn up in its atmosphere.'

Chapter Thirty-One

We were back in the Flex, soaring high over the forests of Canada. Chad and I were in the pilots' seats, although we had the vessel on automatic. Alexi Kozlov was in the rear. We had not handcuffed him this time. We simply asked him to remain seated and we would drop him off to the authorities as soon as possible. He had seemed to accept our change of mind as yet another bizarre event in this endless day.

I peered through the front window at the clear blue sky. It was a beautiful day. People were probably spending time with their families. Some were eating meals. Others were working. The mass of humanity was doing what it always did.

While all that was happening, I was falling apart. The last I had seen of Brodie was the image of her lying on the floor of the Tagaar cell. What had she said to me?

'I'm in a cell—'

Those were hardly famous last words. They were certainly not the final words you wanted to hear from the girl with whom you were in love. I could feel tears filling my eyes. Chad reached over and grasped my arm.

'Don't give up, buddy.'

I shook him off.

Chad persisted. 'Brodie can make it if anyone can. She's a tough girl.'

'She might be tough, but—' A beeping came from the console. I leant forward. 'What is that?'

'It looks like someone's signaling us.' Chad frowned.

'Are we still cloaked?'

'We sure are.' His hand hovered over the controls. 'Should I answer it?'

I peered down at the console. I didn't see how anyone could be communicating with us. Chad had told me this ship was completely off The Agency grid.

I shrugged. 'Let's see who's calling.'

He hit the communicator. 'Uh, this is us—'

I rolled my eyes.

'—uh, who is out there?' he continued. 'Who wants to speak to us?'

The radio crackled. Then a voice came through loud and clear.

'It is your friend, Ferdy.' He sounded as clear as if he were in the next room. 'We will play ball again one day soon.'

'Ferdy!' I exploded. 'How did you—I mean, where are you and how—'

'Others want to speak to you,' Ferdy said. 'Jupiter's largest moon is Ganymede—'

I heard the sound of multiple voices speaking all at once. Then—

'Axel?'

'Brodie?' I could not believe my ears. 'Is that you?'

'It's me,' she replied.

I didn't hear her next words because I was whooping so loudly. I actually started dancing around the small interior of the cabin. Finally Chad had to push me back into my seat so the conversation could continue.

'Axel's lost it,' he said. 'Where are you and what's happening?'

We listened as Brodie briefly explained the events of the last few days. Finally she explained about the falling ship.

'Most of the ship is going to burn up in the atmosphere,' she explained. 'But what remains is going to cause one hell of a mess.'

Ferdy's voice came over the channel. 'The impact of the falling ship will be massive. Not only will everyone on board be killed, but the resulting impact may throw enough dust into the atmosphere to create a new ice age.'

'What do you mean?' I asked.

I fell back in my seat. It took me a few seconds to regain my senses. I leant forward. 'Computer,' I said. 'Trace this signal back to its course.'

A few seconds passed. 'The signal has been traced.'

'Distance?'

'Thirty-seven thousand kilometres.'

'Time to intercept at maximum speed?'

'Twelve minutes.'

'Set a course. Maximum speed.' I punched the communicator. 'Ferdy, put Brodie back on.'

'Axel?' A crackle almost drowned out her voice. 'Are you still there?'

'I'm here,' I said. 'I'm on my way.'

The crackling grew worse. 'What are you going—'

The signal died. Chad examined the console.

'We've lost the signal,' he said. 'What have you got in mind?'

I didn't answer him.

'Okay,' Chad continued. 'Now I'm worried. I need you to speak to me, Axelhead. Tell me what you're thinking.'

'That ship is going to crash and kill everyone on board.'

'And?'

'And I'm going to stop that from happening.'

'Uh…how?'

I hadn't worked that out yet. We traveled in silence until the computer came back to life.

'One hundred kilometers till intercept.'

I turned to Chad. 'You take over the Flex. Make certain Alexi makes it out alive.'

Putting the ship on automatic, he hurried after me into the rear compartment. 'What are you doing?'

I dragged open the back door. The interior of the craft immediately filled with freezing cold air. Alexi looked at me as if I'd lost my mind. Chad slapped a communication device into my hand and I secured it to my ear.

'Saving the world,' I answered.

Chapter Thirty-Two

I was already exhausted and I didn't have the faintest idea as to how I was going to do this, but I knew I had to try. High above, I could see the spacecraft. It was a bright red dot in the sky, growing larger with every second that passed. It was falling fast, leaving a trail of smoke behind it. I could not even begin to imagine what it would be like for the people on board the craft.

Increasing my speed, I flew a slow loop across the sky until I was trailing the falling ship. It was impossible to say how long it would take before it hit the ground. I only knew that their time was running out.

I was thousands of feet behind the craft, then only hundreds, and finally I was flying in its slipstream. Slowly rounding the falling vessel, I focused on creating a platform beneath it. The idea I had was simple. I flew by creating a platform under me. That platform lowered or lifted me through the air. I intended to do the same for the spacecraft.

Except the spaceship probably weighed

thousands of tons and I weighed about one hundred and sixty pounds. So the chances of me succeeding were probably close to zero.

So be it.

I extended the platform, making it larger by the second. Time was running out, but I had to remain completely focused on this if I stood any chance of making it work. The platform grew larger and larger until it lay under the body of the massive ship. Now I focused on pushing upward.

Nothing happened.

The invisible platform was complete. It sat beneath the falling spaceship, but it did nothing when I focused on trying to lift the ship. I knew this would be difficult—probably impossible—but I thought—

I decided to change tact. Moving my attention away from trying to lift the craft, I focused on trying to keep the platform in position. Once again it seemed I was having no effect. Then I heard a groaning sound emanate from the enormous vessel. At the same time I noticed something happening to the outer edges of the craft. They were still molten hot. Now they seemed to be spreading out. They were melting into a wider shape, curving downward almost as if they were trying to collect the air.

Dan.

It had to be him. He was also trying to slow the descent of the craft—and he was having an effect. The craft was slowing. Both our efforts were slowing it, but neither of us was powerful enough to be able to stop it entirely. It was simply too large.

The earpiece crackled. Chad's voice came over loud and clear.

'You're a pain in the ass,' he said. 'Just thought I'd let you know.'

'Shut up.'

I saw the Flex Fighter was descending at the same rate as me and the spaceship. 'I need you to form two holes in your platform,' Chad's voice continued. 'One at each end of the ship. I need it so they're pointing downward.'

'What—'

'Just do it!'

I just had to trust him. I envisioned two holes

in the platform. For a terrifying second the ship started falling more quickly, and then I saw the flame disappear from the sides of the craft. It was as if a candle had been extinguished.

Then in the next second I saw two spouts of fire appear under the ship as if they were rockets.

Yes!

That was exactly what Chad was doing. He had rerouted the heat from the hull—and maybe even added to it—and was firing it directly downward to create two rockets. The ship had slowed perceptibly now, but the ground was still growing closer with every passing second. We had to put all our energy into this if we were to stop the craft from slamming into the earth.

Lots of people's lives were depending on us.

Including Brodie.

Whereas I had been fighting to keep the ship stationery, I now put every ounce of effort into trying to lift it again. My body ached with pain. My head felt like it was going to explode. My vision blurred as I saw the craft growing ever closer to the Earth. Now it was only a few thousand feet.

Then a few hundred.

Lift, I thought.

Lift!

It slowed again. I urged the ship to slow with every fiber of my being. My head felt like it had been placed into a vise. The crushing pain inside my skull was terrible. I watched as the ship slowed once again. It was directly above a farmer's field. I saw the makeshift rockets touch the field and the crop instantly burst into flame.

I put one final bit of focus into lifting the ship—

It slammed into the ground.

An enormous plume of dirt erupted into the air around it. Sections of the ship collapsed instantly. Pieces flew off in all directions. From my height above the ship, it was impossible to tell if the entire craft had been destroyed in the collision with the Earth or if it was still relatively intact. I started towards it.

That's when it happened. I had evaporated the

platform so now all I had to control was my own ability to fly. Except I couldn't seem to see straight. My head was aching terribly. I had to get down to the ground or I would simply fall from the sky. Heading towards a small hill, I was aware that my vision was growing darker with every passing second. Just before I landed, it had narrowed to a slim tunnel filled with only a patch of grass in the center.

Everything went black.

Chapter Thirty-Three

The instant I woke up and opened my eyes, I realized my entire world had changed completely.

My eyes were open, but I could not see.

I was blind.

Lying on my back in the field, my hands raked my face in desperation until I finally touched my eyes in complete horror. My eyes were open—wide open—and yet I couldn't see a thing. It had been a bright sunny day a few minutes before. I was flying towards a hill surrounded by trees. Long grass covered the top. It was into that long grass that I had landed.

It was impossible to determine how much time had passed. It could have been minutes or hours or days. And maybe it made no difference anyway.

I was blind.

A sob rose up within me. I felt like I had been hit by a truck. Every inch of my body ached. The terrible pain in my head had passed, but it had been replaced by a dull pulsing throb. The sensation was worst at the back of my eyes.

Weeping, I fell back into the grass and closed my eyes as tightly as I could. Maybe this was temporary. Maybe it would take a few seconds to pass. Keeping my eyes shut, I counted till I got to sixty before I opened them again.

A wall of inky blackness greeted my vision.

I wiped the tears from my eyes. Somehow, I got to my feet and tried to remember the appearance of the landscape. There had been a patchwork of fields, fences, patches of forest and a thin, curving river. Closing my eyes again, I pressed the palms of my hands into my eye sockets and kept my eyes shut for another minute. I finally opened them again.

The darkness drowned me.

The sound of a blue jay echoed across the field. Further away I could hear the slight drone of a distant engine. The sun felt warm on my skin. A breeze tugged at a stray hair on my brow. An insect bounced off my cheek. The whine of it melted away to nothing.

I wanted to scream.

Somehow I fought the impulse and took a

series of deep breaths. My head still ached, but at least now the rest of my body had eased to a dull throb. Clutching my head, I felt something wet on my hand. It had to be blood. I had probably hit my head when I landed.

Had that caused my blindness?

Maybe this was only temporary. Regardless, I had to move. I had to find Brodie and the others. I had to find out if they had survived the crash or not. Survival was the first order of business. I had to find other people. To do that, I needed to find houses. Roads. Fences.

I started walking. Holding my hands out in front of me, I felt only long grass. My last memory was not of crops. This was simply a grassy knoll in some farmer's field. At some point I would meet a fence. That would lead to another fence. Sooner or later I would come across a person.

Excuse me? Will you help a blind boy?

I wanted to laugh. I wanted to give myself over to peals of laughter and lie down on the grass until I choked to death on my hysteria.

Shut up. I clenched my hands tightly. *Stay focused.*

After the first few minutes I realized I was heading down a gradually sloping hill. I began to feel a little more confident. Encountering a stream would be another good sign. Where there was water there was sure to be people. I just had to—

My left foot met empty air.

Stumbling forward, I threw my hands out and instead something slammed into the left side of my face. For a moment I didn't know up from down. I thought I was being attacked and I punched out wildly. Then I realized I was lying on the ground against some sort of rocky outcrop. A kind of helpless rage consumed me; I had simply fallen over. Crawling away from the stony projection, I encountered soft earth again and I began to pummel it with my fists.

Screaming and crying, I hit it repeatedly until all the energy was gone from my body. At last my head grew dizzy and I fell into another deep silent sleep. There were dreams, but they were the dreams of a sighted boy. He had a girlfriend that he loved, but he should have told her more often. He could see her walking away from him. As she turned back, he saw her lips and her nose and the gentle curve of her cheeks, but she had no eyes.

No eyes.

When I awoke again, I realized I could hear distant sounds. Engines. Voices. I lifted my head slightly. I knew the sound of those engines. They weren't from motor vehicles. They were from—

Helicopters.

Opening my eyes, I saw something move before me. A blur. Grasses.

Light.

I let out a cry. A squeak of astonishment. I blinked a few times. With each blink of my eyes and with each tear that rolled down my face, I found my vision returning. Looking down at my hands, I saw them slowly come back into focus.

I could see again.

Running ecstatically across the field, I followed a helicopter as it disappeared over a stand of trees. Beyond the trees I could see the wreckage of the spacecraft. Somewhere over there was Brodie and the rest of the team. Climbing over a fence, I raced through the sparse wood until I reached the other side.

People were everywhere. Alien beings were everywhere. The army was trying to secure some sort of order. A system was in place, but just barely. At least there were survivors. I pushed through a field of people. I could see ambulances on the other side of the field.

'Axel!'

The voice came from behind me.

Brodie.

Tears filled her eyes as she pushed past two army officers. An instant later she was in my arms and her lips were against mine. After what seemed an eternity, I drew back from her and examined her face. I never wanted to leave her again. I wanted to spend the rest of my life gazing at those beautiful features.

So I did not hear the cry from behind me the first time, and it only registered dimly with me when they spoke again.

'That's him!' the voice said.

I turned. It was Agent Palmer from The Agency. Fury filled her face. Her hand was pointed directly at me. Soldiers flanked her on both sides.

'That's him,' she snarled. 'I want him arrested immediately!'

Chapter Thirty-Four

Morgan Le Fay adjusted the controls on the console and examined the readings. She gave a satisfied grunt. The quantum resonator supplied by the Tagaar was working perfectly. It would still take some time to calibrate the systems, but there was no reason why her adjustments to the Solar Accelerator would not succeed. She stepped back from the equipment.

The inside of the building looked like any high tech laboratory with banks of computer screens lining the walls. The only outstanding feature in the room was the mixing chamber. It looked more like a World War II concrete bunker than something that belonged in a lab. A series of titanium rods like the fingers of a giant hand were located on one side of the chamber. On the other side lay the bowl that accelerated the energy stream. When the Accelerator was activated, the rods would slide across into the chamber and begin the build up to—

A pulsating sound came from outside the building.

Frowning, Morgan stepped from the building into the afternoon light. A Tagaar warship—uncloaked—was coming in to land.

'Now that's something you don't see every day,' she said.

She waited till it had landed and watched Graal and his men disembark. Something had gone wrong. She could see that immediately. Still, there was no reason why her plan would be affected. Graal marched up the stone path to the installation as his men quickly vacated the spacecraft to fan out down the hill.

'Hello, Graal,' Morgan said. 'What a lovely surprise.'

'How are your plans progressing?' he asked.

Always the conversationalist, Morgan thought.

'Very well,' she answered. 'I will be ready in a matter of hours.' She looked past Graal. 'What are your men doing? I thought—'

'Our plans have changed,' he interrupted.

'In what way?'

'The Earthlings know we are here on Earth.

This makes your own weapon all the more important.'

'Thank you.'

'I was not showing gratitude. I was simply stating a fact.' He glanced across the island. 'Our instruments show this island's communications have been cut off from the mainland.'

Morgan nodded. 'I installed a dampening device.'

'Good. My men can hunt in peace.'

What a vicious species, Morgan thought. *It's a shame they look so damn ugly. We could have made a good match.*

The alien followed her into the main laboratory. He glanced around at the equipment, his eyes finally settling on the Tagaar modules that now interfaced with the Solar Accelerator.

'How exactly does this weapon work?' Graal peered closely at Morgan. 'I find it hard to believe a human could create such a device.'

'I've been around.' Morgan smiled sweetly. 'This is an experimental base designed to study the flow of electrons from the sun. For some time the scientists have been experimenting with grabbing a stream of electrons and feeding them into the Accelerator chamber.'

'With what purpose?'

'To supply energy. Once the stream is tethered to the Accelerator, it sets up a continuous link back to its source.'

'The sun?'

Morgan nodded. 'The idea is to accelerate the flow so that an endless supply of free energy is available.'

'It sounds very primitive.' Graal scrutinized the equipment. 'Surely fission is a better system.'

'That technology hasn't been invented yet.'

'I see.' He peered at the quantum resonator connected to the computer. 'And why did you need our equipment?'

'Your device will enable me to boost the input into the chamber and then feed it back at the sun.'

'Meaning?'

'Meaning that I can build a massive explosion

on its surface.' She paused. 'You are probably familiar with an EMP?'

'Electromagnetic Pulse?'

'Exactly. The detonation of an EMP can knock out electricity across an entire city. Once the power fails, so does communication, transport and everything else that holds a civilisation together.' She pointed to the mixing chamber. 'The Solar Accelerator will create an explosion on the sun's surface so massive that electricity across the planet will be knocked out for months.

'The human race will be reduced to savagery. Chaos will reign.'

Graal nodded approvingly. This woman annoyed him with her confidence, but he admired her complete lack of ethics. It was rare to find in a species, and even rarer in a woman.

'Millions will die in the short term,' Graal said. 'And many more millions in the ensuing weeks. When the Tagaar arrive we will be greeted as heroes as we help to 'rebuild' this world.' It was a brilliant plan. A scheme worthy even of a Tagaar. He peered closely at the woman. 'Are you sure you are human?'

'Please,' Morgan tittered. 'A girl's got to have some secrets.'

Chapter Thirty-Five

I was in trouble. Big trouble. No sooner had Agent Palmer seen me than I was arrested and taken to a military vehicle. Chad was already in the back, handcuffed and furious. He looked up as I was pushed inside and handcuffed to the seat opposite him.

'What do they think they're doing?' he demanded. 'We just stopped that ship from crashing. We just—'

'I know,' I agreed. 'We also just kidnapped the Premier of Russia and brought the world to the brink of nuclear war. They might be unhappy about that.'

Chad clamped his mouth shut. He looked like he wanted to say something else, but at that moment a military commander appeared at the doorway of the truck. He was a square-jawed man with a gray crew cut. He looked so solid he could have been carved from granite. A realization slowly struck me as he climbed into the back of the van. He was from the military. The American Military. Most of the people milling around the crashed spacecraft were soldiers.

And Agent Palmer was flanked by soldiers. It seemed that the connections between The Agency and the US Government had become far closer than we could have imagined.

The man sat down on the bench next to me. 'I am General Clarke,' he said. 'And you're the boys who have caused us so much trouble.'

'You should be pinning medals on us!' Chad said. 'Not arresting us.'

'I'd say the chances of you boys receiving a medal are about as likely as Amelia Earhart becoming President.' He shook his head. 'You're both in serious trouble.'

'You can't hold us,' Chad said. 'We can break free any time we want.'

'I know about your powers,' the general said. 'And you know you could simply break free of those handcuffs. You really do have powers far beyond those of mortal man.' He looked at me. 'But trust me when I say that we could retaliate with enormous force. You don't want to have the might of the United States war machine against you.'

'But—' I began.

Clarke held up a hand. 'I know why you pulled this crazy stunt. That's all been explained to me. And it's true you saved thousands of lives today.'

'If that ship had hit the Earth—'

'All right. You saved millions of lives, but you also stole a deadly weapon. You infiltrated Russian airspace. You attacked Russian armed forces. You kidnapped the Premier of Russia, Alexi Kozlov. You—'

'It was me.' I shot a look at Chad. 'It had nothing to do with Chad. I was the one who broke those laws. He had nothing to do with this.'

'We both know that's only partly true,' General Clarke said. 'For any one of those offenses you could go to jail. Considering everything you've done—son, are you all right?'

He was staring at the front of my shirt. I looked down. There was blood on my shirt. I touched my face with my cuffed hands. I was having a nose bleed. Before I could speak, the world began to spin and then everything went dark.

When I awoke I found myself in a hospital bed. I sat up with a groan. My head hurt again. There were other beds in the room, but they were empty. A man hurried in with a chart. It took me a moment to recognize him. Then I realized it was Doctor Williams from The Agency. He had been doing tests to discover why my powers were intermittent. I started to climb from the bed.

'Hey there. Not so fast.'

He pushed me back onto the bed.

'What happened?' I asked.

'You tell me. Apparently you passed out in mid-conversation.'

He asked me a series of questions and wrote down my replies on his notepad. When he asked me if I'd been exerting myself over the last few days, I simply laughed and fell silent.

'Out with it,' he demanded. 'In detail.'

So I told him about the flight to Russia and everything that had happened since. He looked downright worried when I told him about my temporary blindness. When I finished speaking he simply shook his head and laid down the clipboard.

'I was afraid this would happen,' he said. 'Your powers have been in a constant state of flux since you were modified. Now I think you've exerted yourself so much that you've…well…'

'What?'

'You've fried your circuits. You're in danger of giving yourself a stroke, a brain hemorrhage or worse if you continue to use your powers.'

I felt the color drain from my face. 'That's…that's not possible.'

'Not only it is possible, but it's likely.' He shook his head. 'You're a time bomb waiting to happen.'

There was a knock at the door.

'Does that doctor-patient confidentiality agreement—'

'Apply? Of course.'

'Then please keep this to yourself.'

The door opened and Brodie burst in.

'Axel!'

We had our second reunion in as many hours.

She climbed onto the hospital bed and held me close as I contemplated what the doctor had told me. A stoke...brain haemorrhage...was there any good news? I asked her again about the events of the last few days. After she filled me in, she took my hand and looked into my eyes.

'You shouldn't have done it,' she said.

'What? Tried to save you?'

'But the Russian Premier—'

'I couldn't shoot him,' I said. 'I couldn't use the Stonekiller on him. I wanted to, but it just wasn't in me.'

'Good.'

'But I would have done just about anything to save you,' I said. 'You're the girl I love.'

She kissed me again. That made everything worthwhile. Almost.

Tears filled Brodie's eyes. 'We're on the move again.'

'What do you mean?'

'Don't you know—' She stopped herself. 'Of course you don't. We're on board an American

Military Craft called the Helix. It's like a Flex, but about a thousand times larger. We're on our way to Scotland.'

'What?'

'Ferdy was able to hack into the Tagaar communications system for a short time,' she said. 'Before he was cut off, he heard a conversation regarding a woman by the name of Morgan Le Fay.' She went on to explain about the woman's plan to use a worldwide EMP. 'The Tagaar have thrown up a shield around Cargall Island. British forces have tried to break through, but they've failed. They want us to help.' She gripped my hand. 'That includes you.'

'Us? Me?' I rolled my eyes. 'I get to risk my life all over again before going to jail?'

Brodie looked miserable. 'Jail is still on the cards, but this is so serious they're willing to release you. Temporarily.'

'Great.'

She gripped my arm. 'You don't owe them anything.'

'I know.'

'You could break out of here. You could leave and never come back.'

'And what about you?'

Brodie looked down. 'The others need me. This is big. If Morgan Le Fay isn't stopped…it could mean the end of everything.'

The end of everything. On the other hand, if I did help, it might mean the end of me. Still, we were a team. I wouldn't let them face something like this without me. I let out a long sigh, released Brodie and climbed out of the bed. As I struggled my shoes onto my feet, Doctor Williams re-entered the surgery. He looked at me with astonishment.

'What do you think you're doing?' he demanded. 'Get back into bed.'

'No can do,' I said. 'Duty calls.'

'But—'

'I'll take it easy.' I didn't want him spilling the beans about my health. 'I promise.'

Chapter Thirty-Six

My mind whirled with conflicting thoughts as I escaped the sick bay with Brodie and we made our way through the Helix. My place wasn't in a hospital bed. I needed to be with my friends if they were going into action. My head felt better and I wasn't about to exert myself—if I could help it.

The Helix was an amazing vessel. The size of a battleship, it was shaped like an enormous square bug with supporting legs protruding from each corner. It seemed equally capable of both horizontal and vertical flight. I felt a sea of eyes turn to me as we entered the bridge.

It looked like General Clarke had just started giving a briefing to the rest of the team. Chad was there, but didn't look happy. Dan and Ebony looked slightly rebellious. Ferdy—

Well, he looked like Ferdy.

'Axel,' the general said. 'Thank you for joining us.'

I nodded.

'We're on our way to join with NATO forces

to breach the defenses around Cargall Island,' he explained. 'A woman known as Morgan Le Fay has taken control of the island with the Tagaar.'

'Morgan Le Fay?' Ebony frowned. 'Isn't that the name of the woman from Arthurian legend? From the Knights of the Round Table?'

'It is,' the general confirmed. 'It is either a woman using her name—'

'Or it's the real thing,' Chad said. 'She must be old.'

'Very.' Ferdy nodded solemnly. 'Although not as old as Redwood trees—'

'General Clarke,' I said. 'I've got a couple of questions.'

He nodded.

'How does The Agency fit into all this?' I asked.

'The US Government has entered into an arrangement with The Agency,' General Clarke said. 'That organization is now working through us.'

An arrangement? I didn't like the sound of that, but who was I to argue? Within hours I would probably be placed into a cell and wouldn't see the light of day till I was old and gray. If The Agency wanted to enter into a deal with Burger King there was little I could do about it.

'And what's so special about Cargall Island?' I asked.

'Cargall Island houses an experimental device called a Solar Accelerator. Scientists have been trying to develop a free and endless supply of energy. We believe Morgan Le Fay has modified it to produce the Electromagnetic Pulse.'

'But how?' Dan asked. 'And isn't Morgan Le Fay supposed to be a witch? How did she become some sort of super scientist?'

'The Morgan of legend was supposed to be Merlin's sister,' the general confirmed. 'We suspect she's actually some type of alien or modification. Regardless, it appears she has forged an alliance with the Tagaar.'

'General,' an aid called from one of the bridge stations. 'We're approaching Cargall Island.'

He nodded. 'I'll ask you all to remain on

hand. I believe other mods will be joining us within minutes.'

We could see the island growing closer with every passing second from our position on the bridge. It was a tiny speck in the enormous sea. A flotilla of various sea craft were surrounding the island. It looked like they were firing directly at the body of land, but their shots were hitting a pale green dome. Nothing was getting through.

'The barrier looks powerful,' Ferdy said. 'More powerful than the Great Wall of China. The wall was started in the year—'

'Ferdy,' Chad said. 'You got any ideas about how to bring that thing down?'

'Preliminary information suggests that the shield is generated by a squadron of six Tagaar ships in flight around the island,' Ferdy said. 'If any one of the ships can be disabled, it may weaken the dome enough to be penetrated.'

Another group of people hurried onto the bridge. Most of them looked like scientists, but Agent Palmer was with them. She gave me a curt nod.

'How quickly the jailbirds fly their cage,' she said.

Obviously she was still annoyed with us.

At that moment a beam of yellow light sprang forth from the island and pierced the dome. Several people on the bridge cried out as the column of light spat high into the sky and disappeared out of sight.

'Morgan Le Fay has begun the detonation sequence,' Ferdy said, peering at the yellow light. 'Ferdy needs to examine the data coming from the sensors.'

Agent Palmer led us over to a spare console where Ferdy quickly brought up some information. He examined the display.

'How does it look?' I asked.

'It looks like a computer screen, Axel.'

'No. I mean, is there a way through the barrier?'

'There is a way,' Ferdy confirmed. 'There is a small gap surrounding the point where the beam intersects the dome.'

'Is it possible to get through that gap?'

'It would require an expert pilot.'

'I could fly through the hole.'

'If you touched the edge of the dome you would be vaporised,' Ferdy said. 'An aircraft would deliver a margin of safety. There are small fliers on board the Helix known as Atom ships. One of them may be able to fit through.'

The voice came from behind us. 'I can pilot that ship.'

'Mr. Brown!'

The black military man had been my trainer when I first joined The Agency. I had not seen him in months.

He gave me a quick smile. 'I've logged over a thousand hours in Atoms.'

The general joined us and we quickly explained the plan to him.

'All forces will need to attack at the same moment,' Ferdy continued. 'Ferdy believes that may weaken the dome enough to increase the size of the hole. Once the Atom craft is within the dome, bringing down one of the Tagaar vessels may collapse the entire shield.'

The general started barking orders. Ferdy was to remain on the Helix to monitor the readings from the dome. Brodie and Ebony would stay with him. Myself, Chad and Dan would squeeze into the Atom with Mr. Brown at the helm.

It sounded like a plan. Whether it was a good plan or not remained to be seen. As we followed Mr. Brown from the bridge, I felt a hand on my arm.

Brodie.

'You're leaving without saying goodbye?' She looked furious and upset at the same time. 'Don't you have anything to say?'

'I don't need to say goodbye,' I said. 'We'll all meet up on the island.'

By now the others had stopped in the corridor.

'Axel,' Mr. Brown said. 'Will you just kiss the girl?'

So I kissed her. We hurried away down the corridor. I looked back one last time to see her watching me. She gave me a small wave.

Goodbye, she mouthed.

Chapter Thirty-Seven

The Atom zoomed away from the Helix at an incredible speed. I had thought the Flex Fighters were fast, but they had nothing on this. The Atom was built more like a conventional jet, but the three of us were squeezed into a tiny space directly behind the pilot's seat. Mr. Brown did a loop of the dome to get a sense of the area where the pulse broke through at the top.

'I'm not sure I can see a gap,' he said.

'Get Ferdy on the comm,' I said. 'He can give us some direction.'

Mr. Brown communicated with the bridge of the Helix. Ferdy's voice came through loud and clear. After a brief explanation of the life cycle of the Monarch Butterfly, he explained how to best approach the gap.

'It surrounds the exit point of the beam,' Ferdy said. 'It is currently quite small. Only about two meters across.'

'Great,' Mr. Brown said without enthusiasm. 'Atoms have a wing span of six metres.'

'Ferdy will direct the general to start a

simultaneous attack on the dome,' Ferdy replied. 'Be ready to make your final approach.'

Mr. Brown circled around the top of the dome. I could see a multitude of ships in the sea as well as jet fighters and tiny figures in the air.

'I can see other superheroes,' I said. 'A lot of people know how to fly.'

'I wonder if our Russian friends are down there.' Chad peered downward. 'I'm sure they'd love to get together for a game of chess.'

'I'm sure.' I glanced over at Dan. He was very quiet. Actually, he looked quite pale. I diverted my gaze to the windscreen behind him as a slow realization came over me. It was all too easy to forget we were a bunch of teenagers. We might have superpowers, but we still felt fear.

'How are you holding up?' I asked Dan.

He looked at me. 'Fine. Just thinking about what's ahead.'

'I'm a bit nervous,' I admitted.

'Really?'

'I always am when I have to go into a fight.' I

turned to Chad. 'What about you?'

'I'm never afraid,' he said. 'Well…not much…'

'I just don't want to let anyone down.' Dan's eyes were downcast. 'There's so much riding on this—'

'You won't let anyone down,' Chad said. 'Axel might. He freezes up sometimes. Falls apart at the seams—'

I rolled my eyes.

'It's often up to The Chad,' he continued, 'to save the day.'

The Chad?

Ferdy's voice came over the radio. 'The general has arranged for the forces to strike in sixty seconds.'

'Roger that,' Mr. Brown said.

We felt the Atom begin to swing around in another enormous loop over the dome as Ferdy's voice counted down the seconds. Looking over Mr. Brown's head, I could see the yellow beam filling most of the windscreen. That beam was in direct contact with the sun ninety-three million miles away. I didn't want to think about what would happen if we came into contact with it.

'…three…two…one,' Ferdy said.

Even from our position within the flier, we could hear the enormous barrage rise up from beneath us. At the same moment we saw a gap appear in the dome around the beam. I felt the Atom accelerate.

'This'll be close,' Mr. Brown grunted.

We headed straight towards the hole. At the last moment, he seemed to push the Atom into a dive. I felt increased G-forces upon me and then we were through. Suddenly blue sea lay directly below us.

Something flew past the window.

'Watch out—' Mr. Brown started.

Ka-boom!

A missile exploded near the craft and it shuddered wildly in the sky. Mr. Brown rolled the fighter. 'There's a Tagaar vessel closing in on us,' he said. 'I'm returning fire.'

I felt the Atom rock as it fired back at the Tagaar vessel. I could not even see where the alien ship was in relation to our position. We were moving so erratically I could not tell up from down.

'Can you take us closer to the island?' Chad asked.

'I'm trying to do that,' Mr. Brown said. 'Wait—'

He rolled the vessel again and we heard another concussive blast emanate from our aft side. I had an idea, but I needed to see the craft to make it work.

'Mr. Brown,' I said. 'Can you bring us around so we can face the Tagaar ship?'

'Yes, but—'

'Do it!'

Rather than argue, I felt another massive G-force plaster us into our seats. I struggled to speak as the ship cut a wide arc through the sky.

'Chad,' I said. 'When we catch sight of the alien ship—'

'Gotcha,' he said.

He didn't need the plan explained. In the next instant I saw an alien craft appear in the window.

Chad raised his hand and the other ship began to glow. No, not glow. It began to reflect light from the sun as Chad completely enveloped it in ice.

Then it fell from the sky like a rock.

We whooped with delight. Even Mr. Brown punched the air. At the same moment I saw the dome flicker once, twice—and then disappear completely. Chad continued to laugh like a mad person.

'The Chad does it again!' he whooped. 'The Chad—'

He didn't finish the sentence because at that moment a missile struck the wing of the Atom and tore the ship apart.

Chapter Thirty-Eight

'General!' the pilot of the Helix shouted. 'The barrier's down!'

'Take us in,' General Clarke ordered.

Brodie and Ebony grabbed Ferdy and drew him away from the console.

'It looks like this is it,' Ebony said.

'This is what?' Ferdy asked.

'I mean...oh, never mind. Let's just hope we get to the island in one piece.'

'There's an alien vessel closing on us,' the bridge commander announced. 'It's firing.'

'Raise the Grav shields and start our descent.'

It occurred to Ebony that the US government had technologies that no-one else had ever heard about. The Helix was one of those technologies. She wondered how they had kept their equipment a secret for so long. She felt her ears pop as the Helix slowly descended towards the water. At the same time she felt the vessel shudder as missiles from the approaching craft slammed into their vessel.

'The Grav shields are holding,' a lieutenant

announced. 'But a Tagaar ship is closing rapidly.'

Ebony could see the approaching vessel clearer now through the view screen. It was larger than the others she had seen after they were captured by the aliens. The approaching ship was definitely not a fighter craft. Even at this distance it seemed to rival the Helix in size.

'Close weapons on the target and—'

'It's on a collision course!' the lieutenant yelled.

'What?' the general roared.

'Collision course! Range five hundred feet!'

'Fire on it!' General Clarke roared. 'Keep firing until—'

The vessel suddenly disappeared from view.

Brodie and her friends looked at each other.

'Where did it go?' Brodie asked.

General Clarke was asking the same question. 'Location of Tagaar Vessel?'

'It's…it's…not there anymore,' the lieutenant said. 'It's as if—'

The Helix lurched to one side and Brodie

found herself flying through the air. She hit the floor, banging her elbow hard on the edge of one of the consoles. The ship lurched again—this time in the opposite direction. She caught sight of arms, legs, chairs and General Clarke as they tumbled about on the floor of the bridge.

What the hell was going on?

Most of the flight personnel had kept their seats. 'The Tagaar vessel is directly above the Helix,' she said. 'It's attached to us.'

Alarms rang throughout the Helix.

'Boarding…boarding…boarding…' The computer repeated the same word again and again.

'What's happening?' Ebony asked.

'The Tagaar have started to board the Helix,' Ferdy explained.

'In mid-flight?'

The ship shuddered again and this time Brodie heard the sound of firing coming from the corridor. A computer voice started to intone another warning.

'All civilians to evacuation stations…all civilians—'

'That's us,' Brodie said.

She grabbed Ferdy and Ebony and half-dragged them with her as they hurried down a corridor away from the bridge.

'Shouldn't Ferdy and his friends stay and fight?' Ferdy asked. 'The crew of the Helix may need us.'

'The planet needs us,' Brodie said.

They raced down a corridor. Military personnel were dashing in all directions. Brodie grabbed a passing soldier by the arm.

'Where's the evacuation station?' she asked.

He pointed down a vertical ladder leading to the lower decks. They hurried down it until they reached a docking bay for aircraft. Several scientists and other civilians were climbing into egg-shaped escape capsules. These were being ejected from the side of the vessel. Brodie could hear the sound of fighting from the decks above. It sounded like a full-scale war was in progress.

She grabbed the others and they jammed themselves into one of the evacuation pods. It readied itself to fire.

'Ferdy estimates we only have a forty-two percent chance of surviving—'

'Enough with the numbers!' Brodie snapped.

The Helix shuddered again as an ominous groan resounded throughout the body of the ship. Brodie was slammed back into her seat as the egg was ejected from the Helix. Then they were in mid-air and heading rapidly towards the water.

Ferdy activated a panel and a control column shot up from the floor between them.

'Do you know how to fly this thing?' Ebony asked.

'Ferdy has read the manual.' He peered at the controls. 'But there is a problem.'

'What is it?'

'The engines have failed.'

Brodie blanched. 'What does that mean?'

'The chances of surviving a descent into the water are now only twelve percent—'

Their fall was abruptly halted in mid-flight. Brodie swung about and saw a masked face at the side of the capsule. The mask was blue in color and had a small Union Jack above the eyes. The young man behind the mask looked to be about twenty years old.

'What is it?' Ebony screamed. 'What's happening?'

'It's okay,' Brodie said. 'There's a flying…super person at the window. He's got us.'

'Oh, good.'

They watched the island draw closer. Finally the masked man gently placed the escape capsule on the rocky beach. Brodie disengaged the lock and they climbed out onto the pebble beach as the masked hero leapt back up into the sky. He sailed into the distance with his crimson red cape flowing gently behind him, his rear end very comfortably encased within a pair of stretch pants.

'Very nice,' Brodie said.

'You mean the uniform?' Ebony smiled.

'Oh…absolutely,' she said. 'The uniform. We need uniforms.'

They stumbled to their feet. Out at sea the

battle was continuing. The sky had become a mass of fire and smoke. They saw something slowly falling towards the ocean. Ebony cried out in shock.

'That's the Helix,' she said.

Although there had only been five Tagaar warships, it appeared they were all carrying a full complement of fighter craft. There were now hundreds of airborne vessels roaring across the sky. Costumed heroes were in the middle of the fray. Battleships were firing at Tagaar vessels while taking fire from alien ships. At least one cruiser was on fire and sinking.

Their vision was cut off by another barrier of green light.

'What's going on?' Ebony asked.

'It appears the Tagaar have reinstated the barrier,' Ferdy said.

'You mean—'

'We are cut off from the outside world.' He nodded towards the Solar Accelerator at the top of the hill. 'Only Ferdy and his friends can stop the EMP now.'

Chapter Thirty-Nine

I landed us safely at one end of Cargill Island. It had been a tense few minutes as the Atom had fallen apart in mid-flight, but I was able to fashion a flying platform and take us in to the island. Despite a killer headache, my powers had worked fine. Just as we landed on the beach, I heard a hiss behind us as a second dome encased the island.

Mr. Brown was clenching his leg.

'Are you all right?' Chad asked.

'My leg is broken,' Mr. Brown said. 'I don't think I can go on. You'll have to leave me.'

I looked more closely at Dan. He was gripping his arm. 'Is your arm okay?'

'It's fine.'

Chad examined it more closely. 'I'm no doctor, but I think it's broken too.'

'It's not.' He looked angry. 'I can keep going.'

Laying a hand on his shoulder, I said, 'I know you can, but someone has got to look after Mr. Brown.'

'But he can—'

'This island is probably crawling with Tagaar warriors.' I drew him to one side. 'He needs protection.'

Dan nodded. 'Okay, but I'm happy to come if you need me.'

'I know,' I said firmly. 'But we need you to guard Mr. Brown. And yourself.'

Chad and I carried Mr. Brown across the rocky beach until we reached an enclave in the rocks. We placed him inside. I looked up and down the beach. I doubted anyone would see either him or Dan as long as they stayed out of sight. Dan still looked rebellious and annoyed at being left behind.

'We'll be back for you ASAP,' I promised. 'Stay alert.'

Dan nodded. 'Be safe.'

We hurried up from the beach until we reached a clump of trees. I could see a small, winding street with a scattering of houses on both sides. One of the buildings had burnt to the ground. There were dead bodies in the street. Beyond it, the road continued to the installation. The yellow beam of the EMP was growing brighter with every second.

'We're at the right place,' I said.

'I'd say so,' Chad said. 'You know something else, buddy? It's you and me again.'

'The dynamic duo?'

'More like The Chad and…well, Axel.'

I rolled my eyes. 'Let's go.'

We hurried up to the closest house and took shelter on the side away from the installation. The body of an elderly woman lay on the stone path outside. The sight enraged me.

'The Tagaar think they're warriors, do they?' I asked. 'Hard to imagine a harmless old lady putting up much of a fight.'

'They don't know what fighting is,' Chad said grimly.

We hurried up to the next building. I saw a Tagaar warrior marching down the hill behind the group of scattered houses. I wanted to attack, but I fought the urge. Our goal was the Solar Accelerator. We waited until the alien moved out of sight before continuing up the hill. Taking refuge in the ruins of another building, I saw one of the Tagaar warships perched on the hill next to the Accelerator.

Something dripped down my shirt. I was having another nosebleed.

'Are you okay, Axel?' Chad asked.

'Absolutely. I normally save this trick for children's parties.'

'Very funny.' He watched me closely as I pinched my nose. The bleeding stopped after a moment. 'If you need to stop—'

'Let's keep moving,' I interrupted, and hurried away from the building.

We continued up the hill until we reached a stone wall. We peered around it. A wire fence surrounded the installation, but this had been torn down in places. The body of an elderly security guard lay on the ground near the gate.

'I think we're going to make it,' I said. 'Once we get into the building—'

The sound of footsteps came from behind us. We turned to see two Tagaar warriors advancing with weapons ready.

Chad sighed. 'Can't it be easy for once?'

Chapter Forty

Dan watched Mr. Brown as he slept in the rocky enclave. Actually, he was unsure if the man was asleep or unconscious. His face looked pale and his eyes had been shut for several minutes. Dan could imagine how he felt. His left arm was in the makeshift sling, but it was hurting more all the time. Continuing with the others would have been a serious mistake. They needed able-bodied people. Not a short, dumpy kid with a broken arm.

He sighed. It wasn't easy being the youngest of the group.

He stuck his head out of the enclave—and pulled it back in again.

'Hell,' he muttered.

A Tagaar warrior was making his way along the beach. There appeared to be only one of them, but one was enough. He was still some distance away. Dan looked around wildly. Axel and Chad had told him to look after Mr. Brown, but now he was uncertain as to exactly how he was supposed to do that.

Wait a minute, he thought. *Mr. Brown has a gun.*

Dan took it from him gently. It was small but would suffice. He had been trained in the use of several weapons during his time with The Agency. He knew how to fire the weapon, but he wasn't sure how effective it would be against a Tagaar. Of course, he also had his powers. Unfortunately, he was only able to manipulate metal, and there wasn't a whole lot of that around.

He peered out from the gap again. The warrior would be here within moments. It would probably be best to—

A heavy hand landed on his shoulder. He didn't move at first. Then he slowly shifted his head to see a Tagaar soldier standing behind him. Dan gulped. The alien towered over him by about three feet.

Dan tried to keep his voice even. 'Do you know you look like a fish?'

Dan pulled the trigger. The first bullet hit the alien in the stomach. As it raised its own weapon,

Dan fired again and hit it mid-chest. The third bullet slammed into its throat. Green blood poured from the wounds. The alien made a final attempt to speak before collapsing to the ground.

Falling back against the rock, Dan realized his heart was thumping wildly in his chest. The firing of the gun had been like a series of explosions in the small enclave, but Mr. Brown hadn't moved at all. He really was unconscious. Still gripping the weapon, Dan swung about and looked back down the beach.

Empty.

Damn, he thought. *The other warrior must have heard the gun.*

But where had he gone?

Dan stepped cautiously from the enclosure. He still had the weapon raised and he was ready to use it. The entire beach lay deserted. The waves continued to sweep up and down it, tumbling over the stones on the shoreline. He peered towards the hills. The warrior wouldn't have had enough time to move out of sight.

So where was he?

He heard a single splash of water come from the ocean. Turning, he was ready with the weapon, but the Tagaar had made an incredible leap from the water. As well as looking like fish, Dan realized, they were able to behave like them as well. The warrior covered twenty feet in less than a second.

Dan fired until the weapon was empty, but the shots went wide as the Tagaar slammed into him. He hit the ground. Trying to scramble free, he felt the warrior grab his left arm—his broken arm—and lift him into the air.

Aaarrhhh.

The pain was unbelievable. It was so terrible that Dan felt like passing out. But he could not do that. If he did he would die. And so would Mr. Brown. And Axel and Chad were relying on him.

He needed metal. If he had metal, he could turn it into a weapon. Without it—

The warrior laughed. 'You are tiny and weak,' he said. 'Pathetic! We will take over your world and use you as food for our tables.' The warrior stabbed a finger into his chest. 'We are Tagaar. We have—'

'Uniforms made of metal,' Dan suddenly realized, and focused on the armor. The warrior cried out as his uniform started to crush his body. He released Dan in disbelief. Dan hit the sand hard, but he remained focused on the alien. With every passing second the alien's uniform closed around him more tightly until blood poured from a dozen places.

The alien fell to his knees, gave a final choking sound and fell forward on his face.

Dead.

Gasping, Dan settled his arm into the makeshift sling once more and crossed over to Mr. Brown's side. The pain in his arm was terrible, but he was determined to stay conscious.

Mr. Brown opened his eyes slightly.

'Everything under control?' he said softly.

'Everything's fine.'

Dan sat back on the rocks and waited.

Chapter Forty-One

As soon as Brodie and the others saw the alien fighter ship land, aliens started pouring out of the vessel towards them. Ebony formed a metal shield from the air. Brodie had already picked up a length of pipe to use as a weapon. Ferdy grabbed a boulder.

'Ferdy likes to play ball!' he yelled and threw the rock. It knocked over half a dozen warriors.

He grabbed Ebony's shield and they started forward under a hail of weapons fire.

'They wouldn't be so tough without their guns,' Brodie complained.

'I might be able to give us an edge,' Ebony said.

She touched the ground and focused. Brodie watched as it slowly disappeared. Within seconds, she had created a hole a hundred feet deep. Most of the warriors disappeared into it instantly. The remaining few leapt free at the last instant and began to navigate around both edges. Ferdy picked up another rock and took out one of them.

The two remaining warriors sprinted towards

them. Brodie ran forward and flipped one over her shoulder. She slammed a series of punches into him. She had to be fast. Ebony would need her help. The warrior leapt back to his feet and launched a series of punches to her abdomen and face.

Hell, this guy was faster than she expected.

Suddenly a spear flew through his body, impaling and killing him instantly. Brodie swung around to see Ebony standing coolly at her elbow. She had already killed the other warrior.

'Thanks,' Brodie said.

'Any time.'

They rounded the massive hole in the ground and caught sight of two more figures moving towards them. Brodie was ready for another attack, but then she recognized them.

'Axel!' she said. 'Chad!'

Axel threw his arms around her. 'We met some resistance along the way.'

'So did we,' Ebony said. 'Where's Dan?'

Axel explained about the boy's broken arm. At that moment the pulse emanating from the Solar

Accelerator brightened perceptibly. They shielded their eyes from the light.

'It's getting brighter,' Chad said.

'It is,' Ferdy agreed. 'Yellow is a primary colour.'

No-one felt there was enough time to query why this was important, so they crossed the last few feet to the installation. Two ships were now parked near the building: a larger warship, and the smaller fighter craft. Both now appeared silent and still. They hurried around the side of the structure until they found a doorway. Brodie stuck her head through the gap. She was expecting to see a high-tech scientific laboratory. Instead, they seemed to have arrived at the entry to the kitchen. They hurried inside, pulling the door shut behind them. The electricity in the air was enormous. Brodie felt the hair standing up on her arms.

They crossed to the next door. This time she peered through the gap and saw a huge chamber with banks of computer equipment and electrical devices around the edges. In the middle sat a concrete bunker.

Yellow light was pouring from the interior. It seemed to be growing brighter with every passing second.

The room was empty.

'Ferdy,' Chad said. 'You should start to power down that thing.'

Ferdy nodded. He started to examine the controls. A low laugh came from the other side of the equipment. They turned to see a beautiful woman with green eyes slowly approaching them.

'So now they're attacking me with children,' Morgan Le Fay said. 'What a waste.'

Chapter Forty-Two

I could not move.

As soon as the woman looked at me, I found myself frozen to the floor. Only my eyes could move. Glancing at Brodie and the others, I could see they were similarly affected. Ferdy's hand hovered over the control panel. Chad remained in mid-step. Brodie and Ebony were frozen in place.

Brodie's eyes moved about desperately in their sockets. They met mine. I could see pure, naked fear in them.

'Super powered teenagers,' she said. 'Is this the best that humankind can throw at me?'

She shook her head as she slowly crossed to us. 'I've heard of your group. The teenagers from The Agency. I know all about you and your impressive array of powers.' The woman touched Brodie's hair and wrapped it around her fingers. 'You must be Brodie. That's lovely hair, my dear. I believe I will turn it into a teapot warmer.' She smiled. 'When you're dead.'

I wanted to scream at her. I struggled with all

my might to move, but nothing would happen.

The woman stopped again. 'Ebony! You look like a quiet little thing. But what power you have! The ability to transmute objects! My brother Merlin wanted that power all his life, but failed to attain it.' She shook her head. 'Poor Merlin. I had advantages he did not enjoy. My whole life changed when I saw an alien ship fall from the sky one night. When I investigated I found a dying alien in the wreckage. His name was K'charn and he offered me unfathomable power if I would help him live.'

She laughed. 'What did I have to lose? I was a poor, helpless girl who would have ended up marrying some oaf of a farmer if I had refused. So I assisted him, and my life has never been the same since.'

The woman stopped before Chad. I could see him struggling against the woman's power. I saw a rage I had never before seen in him. He wanted to kill this woman and he would have—except he was as helpless as the rest of us.

One muscle, I thought. *Just one muscle.*

I used all my might to move one of my fingers, but it would not move. I tried to use my ability to control air. Nothing would happen. It was as if my power had been switched off. This woman could do anything—and everything—to us and there was nothing we could do about it.

'Chad. The boy of fire and ice,' she continued. 'A beautiful combination. Fire and ice. I traveled to the arctic once with Doctor Frankenstein.' She swept her eyes across us. 'Oh yes. He was real. A brilliant—but sadly deluded—scientist. I went there with him and his pathetic creature. I thought I could learn a new technology that would give me even more power, but it was not to be. I spent three years alone on the ice waiting for rescue.'

She laughed. 'I've led a long and interesting life, but that is nothing as compared to what the future holds for me.' She stood before me. 'Human civilisation will collapse once the detonation occurs, and then I will murder and torture to my heart's content. And then I will move on to the stars.'

The woman gently touched my face. 'And

young Axel. A child of air. Impressive. I believe I will make you suffocate your companions. That should be fun. And then you will suffocate yourself. Do you like that idea?'

I wanted to spit in her face. Instead, I had to watch helplessly as she moved towards Ferdy.

'But now I am disappointed,' she said. 'Here it is. Ferdy. The mental defective of the group. People such as he should be put down. Destroyed. They have no place in this world.' She drew close to his face. 'Can you hear me? You pathetic oaf! You dummy! You will never—'

Ferdy's hand snaked out and grabbed the top of the woman's head.

'Ferdy has friends,' he said. 'Which is more than can be said for you.'

He squeezed hard and pulled upward. As he did so, the top of Morgan's head lifted up—leaving her body behind. Ferdy had a firm grip on her hair. Beneath it squirmed a creature the size of a man's hand. It fought against his grip.

'You   must   be   K'charn,'   Ferdy   said.

'Goodbye.'

He dropped the creature to the floor. Then he stepped on it. It made a bursting sound like an enormous cockroach crushed underfoot.

I immediately felt my free will return. I gasped. The others cried out in relief as we felt the control return to our bodies. I summoned up my power to attack Morgan, but it seemed that retribution was not to be our responsibility. Her beautiful black hair began to turn gray. Her skin wrinkled. Her body sagged.

'No!' she cried. 'No. I am Morgan Le Fay. I am—'

She collapsed to her ground as the aging process overtook over. A thousand years of aging caught up with her in seconds. Giving a final, pathetic cry, we watched in horror as her hair turned white and fell out. Her cheeks grew hollow. Her skin dissipated to nothing. Within seconds she was reduced to bone and dust.

And then only dust.

Chapter Forty-Three

'She was a bad woman,' Ferdy said.

'Weren't you affected by her powers?' I asked. 'The rest of us were unable to move.'

'Really?' Ferdy looked surprised. 'Ferdy thought you were waiting for her to finish speaking.'

'No, we—' I got no further. The building shook beneath our feet and we looked at each other in dismay.

'We need to turn that thing off,' Chad said.

The light in the concrete chamber continued to grow brighter by the second. Ferdy crossed to the console and examined the display as a sound came from outside the building. Ebony and Brodie raced outside while Ferdy manipulated the controls. They returned a moment later.

'That Tagaar warship has just taken off,' Brodie said. 'I think they're running. And it looks like the dome has fallen. Ships and helicopters are approaching the island.'

The entire building shuddered again. Objects fell off benches and clattered onto the floor.

'They should not land,' Ferdy said. 'We need to evacuate.'

'The island?' I asked.

'No,' he said. 'The planet.'

'What?'

Ferdy pointed at the display on the computer screen. 'Morgan Le Fay has miscalculated the power generated by the Solar Accelerator. Her configuration will do more than create a massive EMP. It will ignite the atmosphere.' He examined the controls. 'It will take Ferdy a number of minutes to stop it. There are ships about to land on the island. You must tell them to move away.'

I turned to the others. 'Get everyone away from the island.'

Brodie grabbed my arm. 'But you—'

'I'll be fine,' I said.

The building shuddered again and the intensity of the beam increased. The energy felt like it was burrowing through my skull. Brodie gave me a last despairing look before she hurried from the room.

Ferdy continued to stab at the controls. Finally

he turned to me with fear in his eyes. 'The controls are frozen. Morgan must have built in a failsafe device.'

'Can't it be stopped?'

'Not from here.' He crossed the chamber to the bunker. 'The titanium rods must be manually disengaged from the bowl, but the radiation will kill anyone who enters.'

'We don't need to enter,' I said.

The light from the interior of the chamber was almost blinding, but I could just make out the rods. I focused on bending them away from the bowl. Nothing happened. I looked down at my shirt and realized the entire front of my shirt was drenched with blood from my nose.

No. No. No.

I focused on the metal rods with all my might.

Nothing happened.

Oh no.

Not now.

Please. Not now.

'My powers,' I moaned. 'They're not

working.'

'Then someone must enter the chamber.'

'I'll do in.'

Ferdy looked at me sadly. 'You should not die. You are Ferdy's friend.'

'No one's dying today,' I told him. 'We're all getting out of here together.'

'Unfortunately that won't be possible.'

And that's when he hit me. When I awoke I found myself flat on the floor. It felt like only a few seconds had passed, but the building was shuddering worse than ever. A huge crack had formed in the ceiling. Through it I could see the sky. It had turned a sickly yellow color. I felt the ground shake violently beneath me. An earthquake. Struggling to my feet, I heard glass breaking, and another section of the ceiling collapsed.

Where was Ferdy?

I scrambled across to the bunker. Light poured from the window facing into the chamber. It was more intense than ever, but in the midst of it I could see Ferdy.

'Ferdy!' I screamed.

I fought to open the door. It had been locked from the inside. Again I attempted to use my powers, but nothing happened. I returned to the window, banging on it in desperation. I could see Ferdy pushing against the rods with all his might.

'Ferdy!' I screamed. 'Open the door!'

Through the blinding light, I could just make out Ferdy's figure. He had been horribly burnt by the heat in the chamber. His clothes were smoldering. Most of his hair was gone. He looked up at me.

'Ferdy was able to remotely program the Tagaar fighter ship to intersect with the beam!' he yelled. 'Simultaneously blocking the beam and disrupting the power load may stop the detonation.'

I slammed my fists against the glass.

'The beam is building to ignition,' he said. 'It must be stopped now or the Earth will be destroyed.'

The light built again in intensity and I shielded my eyes.

'Ferdy,' I moaned. 'Get out of there.'

'You told me how you die has got to be at

least as important as how you live.'

Tears were streaming down my face. 'Ferdy...no…no...'

'Ferdy is lucky to—' He stopped. 'I am lucky to have had such friends.'

Then I heard the sound of shearing metal as he put all his strength into bending the titanium rods. The ground shook again as the entire building started to collapse.

'The Tagaar ship is moving into position,' he said. 'There is one chance in 3,472 that—'

Light exploded from the room. A brilliant surge of yellow that infiltrated every crack and every crevice of the structure. In that light was power. A pure burst of energy that threw me backward from the chamber. Hitting the ground, I felt the earth give a final shudder beneath me.

And then—nothing.

Silence.

A final piece of masonry fell from the ceiling and hit the floor behind me. The Solar Accelerator was off. Nothing moved. The terrible shaking of the ground had ended. The brilliant yellow light had disappeared. Stumbling to my feet, I crossed to the concrete bunker. Everything was gone from it. The titanium rods. The bowl. Even part of the floor had been gouged out by the force of the explosion. Everything was gone. Including Ferdy.

Stumbling from the building, I looked up into the sky and saw the terrible yellow light had dissipated. I watched as the Tagaar ship slowly spiraled to earth and landed in the ocean. It looked like it would be underwater within minutes, but I didn't care. I looked beyond it, past the multitude of ships and airplanes, and I saw the distant horizon. A brilliant sunset spanned the sky.

It took me almost an hour to find my friends. They were making their way back from the shoreline with Dan. Mr. Brown lay unconscious on a makeshift stretcher.

'You did it!' Chad raced up to me. 'You saved the world!'

'Ferdy did it,' I said. 'Ferdy saved the world.'

'Where is that little hero?' he asked. 'I've got

to—'

Brodie stopped him with a wave of her hand. She saw the expression on my face as she drew close.

'Axel?' she said.

'Ferdy's gone.' I looked slowly from one face to the next before I told them the news. 'He's dead.'

Chapter Forty-Four

I'd like to say that we were treated like heroes, but it was not to be the case. Certainly, General Clarke and The Agency were pleased that the world had been saved—who wouldn't be?—but too much had happened for everything to go back to normal.

Three days passed before I was called into a meeting with General Clarke. He motioned me to a seat. Armed guards were located both outside his office and on either side of his desk. A lot had changed in a very short time. The alien known as Twenty-Two was nowhere to be seen. We had been told that The Agency would forever be under US government control. What that meant for branches outside the US was anyone's guess. I only knew that this facility, which had once been populated with scientists, was crawling with soldiers. The times were changing. And fast.

'It's time to have a conversation about your future,' he said.

'It's nice to know I have one.'

He did not smile. 'You may not be pleased to

hear what I have to say. You are to be tried by a military tribunal for your crimes.'

'That sounds serious.'

'There are several charges,' he continued. 'Theft of a classified weapon. Invasion of Russian air space. The kidnapping of the Russian Premier.'

'What will all this mean?'

'You're going to jail,' he said. 'You're going to jail for a long time.'

I nodded. I had expected as much. I glanced over at the soldiers. The general caught my gaze.

'I would suggest you adhere to the rule of law,' he said. 'It will go much better for you.'

'And what about Chad?'

'We have been able to minimize his role in this episode. He will receive a severe reprimand, but no charges will be laid against him.'

'Good.' I thought for a long moment. I was pleased about that. He would not have to pay for my actions. 'How long will I spend in prison?'

'That will be up to the judge to decide. I would hope—'

'You mean there's hope?'

The general shuffled some papers in front of him. 'This is the United States. You will be in a clean and well-maintained facility—'

'When?' I interrupted him.

When turned out to be *now*. I was marched back to my room by a team of soldiers where I was allowed to pack a few meager belongings. When I reached The Hub, I found the rest of the team had assembled. They didn't look happy.

'Where do you think you're taking him?' Brodie demanded. Her eyes shone with tears. 'You're not taking him away. He helped to save—'

'Brodie.' I held up a hand. 'It's okay.'

'It's not okay.' She pushed the guards aside and threw herself into my arms and wept. I looked past her and caught Chad's eye. He looked ready for a fight.

He began. 'You've only got to give the word—'

'I know.' The guards shuffled nervously at my side. 'There will be no fighting today. Now we just have to look ahead.'

'To what?' Ebony was crying. 'With Ferdy dead and you gone—'

'You have to make up your own minds,' I said. 'It looks like things are changing around here.'

'But you're part of the team,' Dan said. 'We need you.'

I ruffled his hair. 'Come and visit me. I won't be hard to find.'

Epilog

My first month in prison was the hardest.

A lawyer was assigned to my case. He was a pleasant guy by the name of Phips. I could tell he wasn't too hopeful about the outcome. Whenever I asked him how long it would take for my case to be heard, he always had the same reply.

'These things take time. Could be weeks. Might be months.'

Contemplating the months ahead was probably the least of my worries. It was the years that most concerned me.

The facility I was held in was a maximum security prison in the heart of the Las Vegas desert. There were about a hundred men here—all mods. One was a vampire. Another guy had the strength of five fully grown men. Another guy had six arms. All of them were here for a variety of criminal offenses. Some were thieves. A couple were murderers. They were all destined to spend a long time in jail.

My powers had returned, but they were useless here. Ankle bracelets stifled my abilities. I could not have escaped even if I wanted to.

The days were long and I did my best to stay busy. There was a fully equipped gym that I visited every day, but that was the only place where I mingled with the other inmates. Mostly I read a lot and wrote in my diary. The first book was almost full. Soon I would need another.

I wondered how many I would fill by the time I left this place.

I thought a lot and sometimes I cried. I thought of the friend I had lost. Losing someone makes you realize how your own life has been influenced by them. I would have died at Cargall Island if Ferdy had not stepped into that chamber. The whole planet would have been destroyed if not for him.

He saved the world and no-one even knew.

But would Ferdy have cared? He probably would have said that praise was not important and started spouting some information about the length of a piece of string. That's just how he was.

As one month became two, I was awoken late

one evening by the sound of alarms. The entire prison was surrounded by an electric fence and armed guards. Peering blearily through the bars of my cell, I saw a ship descending from the sky.

A Tagaar fighter ship.

It landed. A section of the vessel opened up and a group of figures burst out into the enclosure. The guards started firing immediately, but a protective ice wall had formed around the ship. As I peered at the guards I saw the barrels of their guns bending backward upon themselves. The figures drew close and one of them placed her hand against the wall of my cell. It turned to air.

A girl stepped inside.

'Brodie,' I said.

'Come on.' She grabbed my hand. 'No ifs or buts.'

I grabbed my diary. She dragged me out of the cell and we hurried across the prison ground. Now the guards had found bigger guns and explosions were happening all around us. We scrambled aboard the alien vessel and Brodie dragged me onto the bridge.

The ship lifted up into the air. It looked like Dan was doing most of the flying.

I looked around in amazement. 'Where did you get this?'

'We stole it,' Chad said. 'You want to complain?'

I shook my head.

Chad stabbed a button and a view screen sprang to life. I watched the lights of the prison grow smaller and dimmer until they faded completely from sight.

'You shouldn't have done this,' I said. 'I'm a criminal and now—'

'If being a criminal is good enough for you,' Brodie said, 'then it's good enough for all of us.'

'Besides,' Ebony joined in. 'We missed you.'

A sob collected in my throat. It was a moment before I could speak.

'So we're all criminals now,' I said. 'On the run from the US government, The Agency and—'

'From everybody,' Dan said.

'So where are we going?' I asked.

'That depends on where Ferdy and his friends want to go.' The voice came from all around me. It seemed to emanate from the ship itself. 'The largest city in Texas is Houston.'

I tried to speak, but no words would come. My mouth fell open in amazement and I saw Chad laughing at me.

'Yeah.' He nodded. 'We looked like that too when it first happened.'

'When—' I was completely lost for words. 'What the hell—'

The voice from the ship continued. 'It is good to see you again, Axel. Ferdy has missed you.'

'Ferdy?'

'Ferdy's body was destroyed in the bunker on Cargall Island,' the voice continued. 'As the chamber exploded, Ferdy's consciousness, his memories—his essence—were caught up in the particles that intersected with the Tagaar warship.'

'So where—'

Brodie put her arm around my shoulders. 'Ferdy's in the ship's computer.'

'He *is* the ship,' Dan said.

Ferdy is the ship. The words went through my head without comprehension. Ferdy had become one with the ship. He was dead, but he wasn't because he was now in the ship's computer.

Ebony spoke up. 'Every thought. Every memory. Every idea. Plus he still plays a mean game of chess.'

'Although throwing the ball around has gotten a whole lot more difficult,' Brodie added.

'Ferdy tried to mention it as a possible outcome of halting the Solar Accelerator,' Ferdy continued. 'The chances of Ferdy's survival were approximately one in 3,472.'

'Those aren't good odds,' I said.

'Ferdy had assistance,' he said.

'What sort of assistance?'

'The will to live,' he said. 'It is a powerful force when someone has friends and family. Possibly the most powerful in the universe. Ferdy did not want to lose the people he loved. It gave Ferdy an edge in surviving that which could not be survived.'

'There's only one problem,' Chad said.

'Which is?' I asked.

'Technically, we're outlaws on a ship.'

'So?'

'So we're pirates.' He shook his head in mock dismay. 'I don't know about you, but I'm not getting a parrot.'

We all laughed. Finally Brodie showed me my position on the bridge. I was seated at a console next to her. There were instructions on the touch display, but as yet they were unreadable.

'It's written in Tagaar,' Brodie said. 'It takes a little getting used to.'

'So where are we going?' I asked.

No-one said anything at first. We all looked at each other in silence before Dan pointed to the view screen. All I could see were stars.

'That-a-way,' he said.

A Few Final Words

I hope you enjoyed reading The Battle for Earth. The other books in the series are:

Diary of a Teenage Superhero (Book One)

The Doomsday Device (Book Two)

The Twisted Future (Book Four)

Terminal Fear (Book Five)

Thanks again and happy reading!

Darrell

CPSIA information can be obtained
at www.ICGtesting.com
Printed in the USA
LVOW03s1453140617
538110LV00010B/516/P

9 781517 122720